LIVING ALONE

Stella Benson

Contents

LIVING ALONE

BY

Stella Benson

This is not a real book. It does not deal with real people, nor should it be read by real people. But there are in the world so many real books already written for the benefit of real people, and there are still so many to be written, that I cannot believe that a little alien book such as this, written for the magically-inclined minority, can be considered too assertive a trespasser.

I have to thank the Editor of the *Athenaeum* for allowing me to reprint the poem "Detachment" and the first chapter of this book. The courtesy of the Editor of the *Pall Mall Gazette* in permitting me to use again any of my contributions to his paper also enables me to include in the fifth chapter the tragic incident of the Mad 'Bus.

    S.B.

THE DWELLER ALONE

My Self has grown too mad for me to master.
Craven, beyond what comfort I can find,
It cries: "***Oh, God, I am stricken with disaster***."
Cries in the night: "***I am stricken, I am blind***...."
I will divorce it. I will make my dwelling
Far from my Self. Not through these hind'ring tears
Will I see men's tears shed. Not with these ears
Will I hear news that tortures in the telling.

    I will go seeking for my soul's remotest
    And stillest place. For oh, I starve and thirst
    To hear in quietness man's passionate protest
    Against the doom with which his world is cursed.
    Not my own wand'rings--not my own abidings--
    Shall give my search a bias and a bent.
    For me is no light moment of content,
    For me no friend, no teller of the tidings.

    The waves of endless time do sing and thunder
    Upon the cliffs of space. And on that sea
    I will sail forth, nor fear to sink thereunder,
    Immeasurable time supporting me:
    That sea--that mother of a million summers,
    Who bore, with melody, a million springs,
    Shall sing for my enchantment, as she sings

To life's forsaken ones, and death's newcomers.

Look, yonder stand the stars to banish anger,
And there the immortal years do laugh at pain,
And here is promise of a blessed languor
To smooth at last the seas of time again.
And all those mothers' sons who did recover
From death, do cry aloud: "***Ah, cease to mourn us.***
To life and love you claimed that you had borne us,
***But we have found death kinder than a lover*.**"

I will divorce my Self. Alone it searches
Amid dark ruins for its yesterday;
Beats with its hands upon the doors of churches,
And, at their altars, finds it cannot pray.
But I am free--I am free of indecision,
Of blood, and weariness, and all things cruel.
I have sold my Self for silence, for the jewel
Of silence, and the shadow of a vision....

CHAPTER I
MAGIC COMES TO A COMMITTEE

There were six women, seven chairs, and a table in an otherwise unfurnished room in an unfashionable part of London. Three of the women were of the kind that has no life apart from committees. They need not be mentioned in detail. The names of two others were Miss Meta Mostyn Ford and Lady Arabel Higgins. Miss Ford was a good woman, as well as a lady. Her hands were beautiful because they paid a manicurist to keep them so, but she was too righteous to powder her nose. She was the sort of person a man would like his best friend to marry. Lady Arabel was older: she was virtuous to the same extent as Achilles was invulnerable. In the beginning, when her soul was being soaked in virtue, the heel of it was fortunately left dry. She had a husband, but no apparent tragedy in her life. These two women were obviously not native to their surroundings. Their eyelashes brought Bond Street--or at least Kensington--to mind; their shoes were mudless; their gloves had not been bought in the sales. Of the sixth woman the less said the better.

All six women were there because their country was at war, and because they felt it to be their duty to assist it to remain at war for the present. They were the nucleus of a committee on War Savings, and they were waiting for their Chairman, who was the Mayor of the borough. He was also a grocer.

Five of the members were discussing methods of persuading poor people to save money. The sixth was making spots on the table with a pen.

They were interrupted, not by the expected Mayor, but by a young woman, who came violently in by the street door, rushed into the middle of the room, and got under the table. The members, in surprise, pushed back their chairs and made ladylike noises of protest and inquiry.

"They're after me," panted the person under the table.

All seven listened to thumping silence for several seconds, and then, as no pursuing outcry declared itself, the Stranger arose, without grace, from her hiding-place.

To anybody except a member of a committee it would have been obvious that the Stranger was of the Cinderella type, and bound to turn out a heroine sooner or later. But perception goes out of committees. The more committees you belong to, the less of ordinary life you will understand. When your daily round becomes nothing more than a daily round of committees you might as well be dead.

The Stranger was not pretty; she had a broad, curious face. Her clothes were much too good to throw away. You would have enjoyed giving them to a decayed gentlewoman.

"I stole this bun," she explained frankly. "There is an uninterned German baker after me."

"And why did you steal it?" asked Miss Ford, pronouncing the H in "why" with a haughty and terrifying sound of suction.

The Stranger sighed. "Because I couldn't afford to buy it."

"And why could you not afford to buy the bun?" asked Miss Ford. "A big strong girl like you."

You will notice that she had had a good deal of experience in social work.

The Stranger said: "Up till ten o'clock this morning I was of the leisured classes like yourselves. I had a hundred pounds."

Lady Arabel was one of the kindest people in the world, but even she quivered at the suggestion of a common leisure. The sort of clothes the Stranger wore Lady Arabel would have called "too dretful." If one is well dressed one is proud, and may look an angel in the eye. If one is really shabby one is even prouder, one often goes out of one's way to look angels in the eye. But if one wears a squirrel fur "set," and a dyed dress that originally cost two and a half guineas, one is damned.

"You have squandered all that money?" pursued Miss Ford.

"Yes. In ten minutes."

A thrill ran through all six members. Several mouths watered.

"I am ashamed of you," said Miss Ford. "I hope the baker will catch you. Don't you know that your country is engaged in the greatest conflict in history? A hundred pounds ... you might have put it in the War Loan."

"Yes," said the Stranger, "I did. That's how I squandered it."

Miss Ford seemed to be partially drowned by this reply. One could see her wits fighting for air.

But Lady Arabel had not committed herself, and therefore escaped this disaster. "You behaved foolishly," she said. "We are all too dretfully anxious to subscribe what we can spare to the War Loan, of course. But the State does not expect more than that of us."

"God bless it," said the Stranger loudly, so that everybody blushed. "Of course it doesn't. But it is fun, don't you think, when you are giving a present, to exceed expectations?"

"The State--" began Lady Arabel, but was nudged into silence by Miss Ford. "Of course it's all untrue. Don't let her think we believe her."

The Stranger heard her. Such people do not only hear with their ears. She laughed.

"You shall see the receipt," she said.

Out of her large pocket she dragged several things before she found what she sought. The sixth member noticed several packets labelled MAGIC, which the Stranger handled very carefully. "Frightfully explosive," she said.

"I believe you're drunk," said Miss Ford, as she took the receipt. It really was a War Loan receipt, and the name and address on it were: "Miss Hazeline Snow, The Bindles, Pymley, Gloucestershire."

Lady Arabel smiled in a relieved way. She had not long been a social worker, and had not yet acquired a taste for making fools of the undeserving. "So this is your name and address," she said.

"No," said the Stranger simply.

"This is your name and address," said Lady Arabel more loudly.

"No," said the Stranger. "I made it up. Don't you think 'The Bindles, Pymley,' is too darling?"

"Quite drunk," repeated Miss Ford. She had attended eight committee meetings that week.

"S--s--s--sh, Meta," hissed Lady Arabel. She leaned forward, not smiling, but pleasantly showing her teeth. "You gave a false name and address. My dear, I wonder if I can guess why."

"I dare say you can," admitted the Stranger. "It's such fun, don't you think, to get no thanks? Don't you sometimes amuse yourself by sending postal orders to people whose addresses look pathetic in the telephone book, or by forgetting to take away the parcels you have bought in poor little shops? Or by standing and looking with ostentatious respect at boy scouts on the march, always bearing in mind that these, in their own eyes, are not little boys trotting behind a disguised curate, but British Troops on the Move? Just two pleased eyes in a crowd, just a hundred pounds dropped from heaven into poor Mr. Bonar Law's wistful hand...."

Miss Ford began to laugh, a ladylike yet nasty laugh. "You amuse me," she said, but not in the kind of way that would make anybody wish to amuse her often.

Miss Ford was the ideal member of committee, and a committee, of course, exists for the purpose of damping enthusiasms.

The Stranger's manners were somehow hectic. Directly she heard that laughter the tears came into her eyes. "Didn't you like what I was saying?" she asked. Tears climbed down her cheekbones.

"Oh!" said Miss Ford. "You seem to be--if not drunk--suffering from some form of hysteria."

"Do you think youth is a form of hysteria?" asked the Stranger. "Or hunger? Or magic? Or--"

"Oh, don't recite any more lists, for the Dear Sake!" implored Miss Ford, who had caught this rather pretty expression where she caught her laugh and most of her thoughts--from contemporary fiction. She had a lot of friends in the writing trade. She knew artists too, and an actress, and a lot of people who talked. She very nearly did something clever herself. She continued: "I wish you could see yourself, trying to be uplifting between the munches of a stolen bun. You'd laugh too. But perhaps you never laugh," she added, straightening her lips.

"How d'you mean--laugh?" asked the Stranger. "I didn't know that noise was called laughing. I thought you were just saying 'Ha--ha.'"

At this moment the Mayor came in. As I told you, he was a grocer, and the Chairman of the committee. He was a bad Chairman, but a good grocer. Grocers generally wear white in the execution of their duty, and this fancy, I think, reflects their pureness of heart. They spend their days among soft substances most beautiful to touch; and sometimes they sell honest-smelling soaps; and sometimes they chop cheeses, and thus reach the glory of the butcher's calling, without its painfulness. Also they handle shining tins, marvellously illustrated.

Mayors and grocers were of course nothing to Miss Ford, but Chairmen were very important. She nodded curtly to the Mayor and grocer, but she pushed the seventh chair towards the Chairman.

"May I just finish with this applicant?" she asked in her thin inclusive committee voice, and then added in the direction of the Stranger: "It's no use talking nonsense. We all see through you, you cannot deceive a committee. But to a certain extent we believe your story, and are willing, if the case proves satisfactory, to give you a helping hand. I will take down a few particulars. First your name?"

"M--m," mused the Stranger. "Let me see, you didn't like Hazeline Snow much, did you? What d'you think of Thelma ... Thelma Bennett Watkins?... You know, the Rutlandshire Watkinses, the younger branch----"

Miss Ford balanced her pen helplessly. "But that isn't your real name."

"How d'you mean--real name?" asked the Stranger anxiously. "Won't that do? What about Iris ... Hyde?... You see, the truth is, I was never actually christened ... I was born a conscientious objector, and also----"

"Oh, for the Dear Sake, be silent!" said Miss Ford, writing down "Thelma Bennett Watkins," in self-defence. "This, I take it, is the name you gave at the time of the National Registration."

"I forget," said the Stranger. "I remember that I put down my trade as Magic, and they registered it on my card as 'Machinist.' Yet Magic, I believe, is a starred profession."

"What is your trade really?" asked Miss Ford.

"I'll show you," replied the Stranger, unbuttoning once more the flap of her pocket.

*   *   *   *   *

She wrote a word upon the air with her finger, and made a flourish under the word. So flowery was the flourish that it span her round, right round upon her toes, and she faced her watchers again. The committee jumped, for the blind ran up, and outside the window, at the end of a strange perspective of street, the trees of some far square were as soft as thistledown against a lemon-coloured sky. A sound came up the street....

The forgotten April and the voices of lambs pealed like bells into the room....

Oh, let us flee from April! We are but swimmers in seas of words, we members of committees, and to the song of April there are no words. What do we know, and what does London know, after all these years of learning?

Old Mother London crouches, with her face buried in her hands; and she is walled in with her fogs and her loud noises, and over her head are the heavy beams of her dark roof, and she has the barred sun for a skylight, and winds that are but hideous draughts rush under her door. London knows much, and every moment she learns a new thing, but this she shall never learn--that the sun shines all day and the moon all night on the silver tiles of her dark house, and that the young months climb her walls, and run singing in and out between her chimneys....

*   *   *   *   *

Nothing else happened in that room. At least nothing more important than the ordinary manifestations attendant upon magic. The lamp had tremulously gone out. Coloured flames danced about the Stranger's head. One felt the thrill of a purring cat against one's ankles, one saw its green eyes glare. But these things hardly counted.

It was all over. The Mayor was heard cracking his fingers, and whispering "Puss, Puss." The lamp relighted itself. Nobody had known that it was so gifted.

The Mayor said: "Splendid, miss, quite splendid. You'd make a fortune on the stage." His tongue, however, seemed to be talking by itself, without the assistance of the Mayor himself. One could see that he was shaken out of his usual grocerly calm, for his feverish hand was stroking a cat where no cat was.

Black cats are only the showy properties of magic, easily materialised, even by beginners, at will. It must be confusing for such an orderly animal as the cat to exist in this intermittent way, never knowing, so to speak, whether it is there or not there, from one moment to another.

The sixth member took a severely bitten pen from between her lips, and said: "Now you mention it, I think I'll go down there again for the week-end. I can pawn my ear-rings."

Nobody of course took any notice of her, yet in a way her remark was logical. For that singing Spring that had for a moment trespassed in the room had reminded her of very familiar things, and for a few seconds she had stood upon a beloved hill, and had looked down between beech trees on a far valley, like a promised land; and had seen in the valley a pale river and a dark town, like milk and honey.

As for Miss Ford, she had become rather white. Although the blind had now pulled itself down, and dismissed April, Miss Ford continued to look at the window. But she cleared her throat and said hoarsely: "Will you kindly answer my questions? I asked you what your trade was."

"It's too dretful of me to interrupt," said Lady Arabel suddenly. "But, do you know, Meta, I feel we are wasting this committee's time. This young person needs no assistance from us." She turned to the Stranger, and added: "My dear, I am dretfully ashamed. You must meet my son Rrchud.... My son Rrchud knows...."

She burst into tears.

The Stranger took her hand.

"I should like awfully to meet Rrchud, and to get to know you better," she said. She grew very red. "I say, I should be awfully pleased if you would call me Angela."

It wasn't her name, but she had noticed that something of this sort is always said when people become motherly and cry.

Then she went away.

"Lawdy," said the Mayor. "I didn't expect she'd go out by the door, somehow. Look--she's left some sort of hardware over there in the corner."

It was a broomstick.

CHAPTER II
THE COMMITTEE COMES TO MAGIC

I don't suppose for a moment that you know Mitten Island: it is a difficult place to get to; you have to change 'buses seven times, going from Kensington, and you have to cross the river by means of a ferry. On Mitten Island there is a model village, consisting of several hundred houses, two churches, and one shop.

It was the sixth member who discovered, after the committee meeting, that the address on the forsaken broomstick's collar was: Number 100 Beautiful Way, Mitten Island, London.

The sixth member, although she was a member of committees, was neither a real expert in, nor a real lover of, Doing Good. In Doing Good, I think, we have got into bad habits. We try in groups to do good to the individual, whereas, if good is to be done, it would seem more likely, and more consonant with precedent, that the individual might do it to the group. Without the smile of a Treasurer we cannot unloose our purse-strings; without the sanction of a Chairman we have no courage; without Minutes we have no memory. There is hardly one of us who would dare to give a flannelette nightgown to a Factory Girl who had Stepped Aside, without a committee to lay the blame on, should the Factory Girl, fortified by the flannelette nightgown, take Further Steps Aside.

The sixth member was only too apt to put her trust in committees. Herself she did not trust at all, though she thought herself quite a good creature, as selves go. She had come to London two years ago, with a little trunk and a lot of good intentions as her only possessions, and she had paid the inevitable penalty for her earnestness. It is a sad thing to see any one of naturally healthy and rebellious tendency stray into the flat path of Charity. Gay heedless young people set their unwary feet between the flowery borders of that path, the thin air of resigned thanks breathed by the deserving poor mounts to their heads like wine; committees lie in wait for them on every side; hostels and settlements entice them fatally to break their journey at every mile; they run rejoicing to their doom, and I think shall eventually find themselves without escape, elected eternal life-members of the Committee that sits around the glassy sea.

The sixth member was saved by a merciful inefficiency of temperament from attaining the vortex of her whirlpool of charity. To be in the vortex is, I believe, almost always to see less. The bull's eye is generally blind.

The sixth member was a person who, where Social Work was concerned, did more or less as she was told, without doing it particularly well. The result, very properly, was that all the work which a committee euphemistically calls "organising work" was left to her. Organising work consists of sitting in 'buses bound for remote quarters of London, and ringing the bells of people who are almost always found to be away for a fortnight. The sixth member had been ordered to organise the return of the broomstick to its owner.

Perhaps it would be more practical to call the sixth member Sarah Brown.

The bereaved owner of the broomstick was washing her hair at Number 100 Beautiful Way, Mitten Island. She was washing it behind the counter of her shop. She was the manageress of the only shop on Mitten Island. It was a general shop, but made a speciality of such goods as Happiness and Magic. Unfortunately Happiness is rather difficult to get in war-time. Sometimes there was quite a queue outside the shop when it opened, and sometimes there was a card outside, saying politely: "Sorry, it's no use waiting. I haven't any." Of course the shop also sold Sunlight Soap, and it was with Sunlight Soap that the shop-lady was washing her hair, because it was Sunday, and this was a comparatively cheap amusement. She had no money. She had meant to go down to the offices of her employer after breakfast, to borrow some of the salary that would be due to her next week. But then she found that she had left her broomstick somewhere. As a rule Harold--for that was the broomstick's name--was fairly independent, and could find his way home alone, but when he got mislaid and left in strange hands, and particularly when kindly finders took him to Scotland Yard, he often lost his head. You, in your innocence, are suggesting that his owner might have borrowed another broomstick from stock.

But you have no idea what arduous work it is, breaking in a wild broomstick to the saddle. It sometimes takes days, and is not really suitable work for a woman, even in war-time. Often the brutes are savage, and always they are obstinate. The shop-lady could not afford to go to the City by Tube, not to mention the ferry fare, which was rather expensive and erratic, not being L.C.C. Of course a flash of lightning is generally available for magic people. But it is considered not only unpatriotic but bad form to use lightning in war-time.

The shop was not expecting customers on Sunday, but its manageress had hardly got her head well into the basin when somebody entered. She stood up dripping.

"Is Miss Thelma Bennett Watkins at home?" asked Sarah Brown, after a pause, during which she made her characteristic effort to remember what she had come for.

"No," said the other. "But do take a seat. We met last night, you may remember. Perhaps you wouldn't mind lending me one-and-twopence to buy two chops for our luncheon. I've got an extra coupon. There's tinned salmon in stock, but I don't advise it."

"I've only got sevenpence, just enough to take me home," answered Sarah Brown. "But I can pawn my ear-rings."

I dare say you have never been in a position to notice that there is no pawn-shop on Mitten Island. The inhabitants of model villages always have assured incomes and pose as lilies of the field. Sarah Brown and her hostess sat down on the counter without regret to a luncheon consisting of one orange, found by the guest in her bag and divided, and two thin captain biscuits from stock. They were both used to dissolving visions of impossible chops, both were cheerfully familiar with the feeling of light tragedy which invades you towards six o'clock P.M., if you have not been able to afford a meal since breakfast.

"Now look here," said Sarah Brown, as she plunged her pocket-knife into the orange. "Would you mind telling me--are you a fairy, or a third-floor-back, or anything of that sort? I won't register it, or put it on the case-paper, I promise, though if you are superhuman in any way I shall be seriously tempted."

"I am a Witch," said the witch.

Now witches and wizards, as you perhaps know, are people who are born for the first time. I suppose we have all passed through this fair experience, we must all have had our chance of making magic. But to most of us it came in the boring beginning of time, and we wasted our best spells on plesiosauri, and protoplasms, and angels with flaming swords, all of whom knew magic too, and were not impressed. Witches and wizards are now rare, though not so rare as you think. Remembering nothing, they know nothing, and are not bored. They have to learn everything from the very beginning, except magic, which is the only really original sin. To the magic eye, magic alone is commonplace, everything else is unknown, unguessed, and undespised. Magic people are always obvious--so obvious that we veteran souls can rarely understand them,--they are never subtle, and though they are new, they are never Modern. You may tell them in your cynical way that to-day is the only real day, and that there is nothing more unmentionable than yesterday except the day before. They will admire your cleverness very much, but the next moment you will find the witch sobbing over Tennyson, or the wizard smiling at the quaint fancies of Sir Edwin Landseer. You cannot really stir up magic people with ordinary human people. You and I have climbed over our thousand lives to a too dreadfully subtle eminence. In our day--in our many days--we have adored everything conceivable, and now we have to fall back on the inconceivable. We stand our idols on their heads, it is newer to do so, and we think we prefer them upside down. Talking constantly, we reel blindfold through eternity, and perhaps if we are lucky, once or twice in a score of lives, the blindfolding handkerchief slips, and we wriggle one eye free, and see gods like trees walking. By Jove, that gives us enough to talk about for two or three lives! Witches and wizards are not blinded by having a Point of View. They just look, and are very much surprised and interested.

All witches and wizards are born strangely and die violently. They are descended always from old mysterious breeds, from women who wrought domestic magic and perished for its sake, and from men who wrought other magic among lost causes and wars without gain, and fell and died, still surprised, still interested, with their faces among flowers. All men who die so are not wizards, nor are all martyred and adventuring women witches, but all such bring a potential strain of magic into their line.

"A witch," said Sarah Brown. "Of course. I have been trying to remember what broomsticks reminded me of. A witch, of course. I have always wished to be friends with a witch."

The witch was unaware that the proper answer to this was: "Oh, my Dear, ***do*** let's. Do you know I had quite a ***crush*** on you from the first minute." She did not answer at all, and Sarah Brown, who was tired of proper answers, was not sorry. Nevertheless the pause seemed a little empty, so she filled it herself, saying pedantically: "Of course I don't believe friendship is an end in itself. Only a means to an end."

"I don't know what you mean," said the witch, after wrestling conscientiously with this remark for a minute. "Do tell me--do you know yourself, or are you just saying it to see what it means?"

Sarah Brown was obviously damped by this, and the witch added kindly: "I bet you twopence you don't know what this place is."

"A shop," said Sarah Brown, who was sitting on the counter.

"It is a sort of convent and monastery mixed," replied the witch. "I am connected with it officially. I undertook to manage it, yet I forget what the proper word for me is. Not undertaker, is it?"

"Superintendent or secretary," suggested Sarah Brown moodily.

"Superintendent, I think," said the witch. "At least I know Peony calls me Soup. Do you live alone?"

"Yes."

"Then you ought to live here. This is the only place in the world of its kind. The name of this house is Living Alone. I'll read you the prospectus."

She fell suddenly upon her knees and began fighting with a drawer. The drawer was evidently one of the many descendants of the Sword Excalibur--none but the appointed hand could draw it forth. The witch, after a struggle, passed this test, and produced a parchment covered with large childish printing in red ink.

"My employer made up this," said the witch. "And the ferryman wrote it out for us."

This is the prospectus:

The name of this house is Living Alone.

It is meant to provide for the needs of those who dislike hotels,

clubs, settlements, hostels, boarding-houses, and lodgings only

less than their own homes; who detest landladies, waiters,

husbands and wives, charwomen, and all forms of lookers after. This house is a monastery and a convent for monks and nuns dedicated to unknown gods. Men and women who are tired of being laboriously kind to their bodies, who like to be a little uncomfortable and quite uncared for, who love to live from week to week without speaking, except to confide their destinations to 'bus-conductors, who are weary of woolly decorations, aspidistras, and the eternal two generations of roses which riot among blue ribbons on hireling wall-papers, who are ignorant of the science of tipping and thanking, who do not know how to cook yet hate to be cooked for, will here find the thing they have desired, and something else as well.

There are six cells in this house, and no common sitting-room. Guests wishing to address each other must do so on the stairs, or in the shop. Each cell has whitewashed walls, and contains a small deal table, one wooden chair, a hard bed, a tin bath, and a little inconvenient fireplace. No guest may bring into the house more than can be carried out again in one large suit-case. Carpets, rugs, mirrors, and any single garment costing more than three guineas, are prohibited. Any guest proved to have made use of a taxi, or to have travelled anywhere first class, or to have bought cigarettes or sweets costing more than three shillings a hundred or eighteenpence a pound respectively, or to have paid more than three and sixpence (war-tax included) for a seat in any place of entertainment, will be instantly expelled. Dogs, cats, goldfish, and other superhuman companions are encouraged.

Working guests are preferred, but if not at work, guests must spend at least eighteen hours out of the twenty-four entirely alone. No guest may entertain or be entertained except under special license obtainable from the Superintendent.

There is a pump in the back yard. There is no telephone, no

electric light, no hot water system, no attendance, and no modern comfort whatever. Tradesmen are forbidden to call. There is no charge for residence in this house.

"It certainly sounds an unusual place," admitted Sarah Brown. "Is the house always full?"

"Never," said the witch. "A lot of people can swallow everything but the last clause. We have at present one guest, called Peony."

She replaced the prospectus in the drawer, which she then tried to shut. While she was engaged in this thundering endeavour, Sarah Brown noticed that the drawer was full of the little paper packets which she had seen the day before in the witch's possession.

"What do you do with your magic?" she asked.

"Oh, many things. Chiefly I use it as an ingredient for happiness, sometimes to remind people, and sometimes to make them forget. It seems to me that some people take happiness rather tragically."

"I find," said Sarah Brown, rather sententiously, "that I always owe my happiness to earth, never to heaven."

"How d'you mean heaven?" said the witch. "I know nothing about heaven. When I used to work in the City, I bought a little book about heaven to read in the Tube every morning. I thought I should grow daily better. But I couldn't see that I did."

Sarah Brown was naturally astonished to meet any one who did not know all about heaven. But she continued the pursuit of her ideas on happiness. Sarah Brown meant to write a book some day, if she could find a really inspiring exercise-book to start in. She thought herself rather good at ideas--poor Sarah Brown, she simply had to be confident about something. She was only inwardly articulate, I think, not outwardly at all, but sometimes she could talk about herself.

"Heaven has given me wretched health, but never gave me youth enough to make the wretchedness adventurous," she went on. "Heaven gave me a thin skin, but never gave me the natural and comforting affections. Heaven probably meant to make a noble woman of me by encrusting me in disabilities, but it left out the necessary nobility at the last moment; it left out, in fact, all the compensations. But luckily I have found the compensations for myself; I just had to find something.

Men and women have given me everything that such as I could expect. I have never met with reasonless enmity, never met with meanness, never met with anything more unbearable than natural indifference, from any man or woman. I have been, I may say, a burden and a bore all over the world; I have been an ill and fretful stranger within all men's gates; I have asked much and given nothing; I have never been a friend. Nobody has ever expected any return from me, yet nothing was grudged. Landladies, policemen, chorus girls, social bounders, prostitutes, the natural enemies, one would say, of such as I, have given me kindness, and often much that they could not easily spare, and always amusement and distraction...."

"Ah, how you interest and excite me," said the witch, whose attention had been frankly wandering. "You are exactly the sort of person we want in this house."

"But--ill?" said Sarah Brown pessimistically. "Oh, witch, I have been so wearisome to every one, so constantly ill. The first thing I get to know about a new hostess or a landlady is always the colour of her dressing-gown by candlelight, or whether she has one."

"Illnesses are never bad here," said the witch. "I bet you twopence I've got something in the shop that would make you well. Three fingers of happiness, neat and hot, at night--"

"But, witch--oh, witch--this is the worst of all. My ears are failing me--I think I am going deaf...."

"You can hear what I say," said the witch.

"Yes, I can hear what you say, but when most people talk I am like a prisoner locked up; and every day there are more and more locked doors between me and the world. You do not know how horrible it is."

"Oh, well," said the witch, "as long as you can hear magic you will not lack a key to your prison. Sometimes it's better not to hear the other things. You are the ideal guest for the House of Living Alone."

"I'll go and fetch David my Dog and Humphrey my Suit-case," said Sarah Brown.

At that moment a taxi was heard to arrive at the other side of the ferry, and the ferryman's voice was heard shouting: "All right, all right, I'll be there in half a tick."

"I hope this isn't Peony in a taxi," said the witch. "I get so tired of expelling guests. She's been drawing her money, which may have been tempting."

They listened.

They heard someone alight from the ferry-boat, and the voice of Miss Meta Mostyn Ford asking the ferryman: "Do you know anything about a young woman of the name of Watkins, living at Number 100 Beautiful Way----"

"No, he doesn't," shouted the witch, opening the shop door. "But do step in. We met yesterday, you may remember. I'll ask the ferryman to get half-a-dozen halfpenny buns for tea, if you will be so kind as to lend me threepence. We don't bake ourselves."

"I have had tea, thank you," said Miss Ford. "I have just come from a little gathering of friends on the other side of the river, and I thought I would call here on my way home. I had noted your address----"

She started as she came in and saw Sarah Brown, and added in her committee voice: "I had noted your address, because I never mind how much trouble I take in following up a promising case."

Sarah Brown, on first hearing that trenchant voice, had lost her head and begun to hide under the counter. But the biscuit-tins refused to make room, so she drew herself up and smiled politely.

"How good of you to go to a little gathering of friends," said the witch, obviously trying to behave like a real human person. "I never do, except now and then by mistake. And even then I only stay when there are grassy sandwiches to eat. Once there were grassy sandwiches mixed with bits of hard-boiled egg, and then I stayed to supper. You didn't have such luck, I see, or you would look happier."

"I don't go to my friends for their food, but for their ideas," said Miss Ford.

Sarah Brown was gliding towards the door.

"Oh, don't go," said the witch, who did not recognise tact when she met it. "I have sent Harold the Broomstick for your Dog David and your Suit-case Humphrey. He is an excellent packer and very clean in his person and work. Please, please, don't go. Do you know, I live in constant dread of being left alone with a clever person."

"I must apologise for my intrusion, in that case," said Miss Ford, with dignity. "I repeat, I only came because I saw yours was an exceptional case."

There was a very long silence in the growing dusk. The moon could already be seen through the glass door, rising, pushing vigorously aside the thickets of the crowded sky. A crack across the corner of the glass was lighted up, and looked like a little sprig of lightning, plucked from a passing storm and preserved in the glass.

Miss Ford suddenly began to talk in a very quick and confused way. Any sane hearer would have known that she was talking by mistake, that she was possessed by some distressingly Anti-Ford spirit, and that nothing she might say in parenthesis like this ought to be remembered against her.

"Oh, God," said Miss Ford, "I have come because I am hungry, hungry for what you spoke of last night, in the dark.... You spoke of an April sea--clashing of cymbals was the expression you used, wasn't it? You spoke of a shore of brown diamonds flat to the ruffled sea ... and white sandhills under a thin veil of grass ... and tamarisks all blown one way...."

"Well?" said the witch.

"Well," faltered Miss Ford. "I think I came to ask you ... whether you knew of nice lodgings there ... plain wholesome bath ... respectable cooking, hot and cold ..."

Her voice faded away pathetically.

There was a sudden shattering, as the door burst open, and a dog and a suit-case were swept in by a brisk broomstick.

"I am so sorry, Miss Watkins," said Miss Ford stiffly. Her face was scarlet--neat and formal again now, but scarlet.--"I am so sorry if I have talked nonsense. I am rather run down, I think, too much work, four important meetings yesterday. I sometimes think I shall break down. I have such alarming nerve-storms."

She looked nervously at Sarah Brown. It is always tiresome to meet fellow-members of committees in private life, especially if one is in a mood for having nerve-storms. People may be excellent in a philanthropic way, of course, and yet impossible socially.

But Sarah Brown had heard very little. She always found Miss Ford's voice difficult. She was on her knees asking her dog David what it had felt like, coming. But David was still too much dazed to say much.

"You must not think," said Miss Ford, "that because I am a practical worker I have no understanding of Inner Meanings. On the contrary, I have perhaps wasted too much of my time on spiritual matters. That is why I take quite a personal and special interest in your case. I had a great friend, now in the trenches, alas, who possessed Power. He used to come to my Wednesdays--at least I used to invite him to come, but he was dreamy like you and constantly mistook the date. He helped me enormously, and I miss him.... Well, the truest charity should be anything but formal, I think, and I saw at a glance that your case was exceptional, and that you also were Occult----"

"How d'you mean--occult?" asked the witch. "Do you mean just knowing magic?"

"A strange mixture," mused Miss Ford self-consciously. It is impossible to muse aloud without self-consciousness. "A strange and rather interesting mixture of naivete and power. The question is--power to what extent? Miss Watkins, I want you to come to one of my Wednesdays to meet one or two people who might possibly help you to a job--lecturing, you know. Lectures on hypnotism or spiritualism, with experiments, are always popular. You certainly have Power, you only want a little advertisement to be a real help to many people."

"How d'you mean--advertisement?" asked the witch. "This new advertisement stunt is one of the problems that tire my head. I am awfully worried by problems. The world seems to be ruled by posters now. People look to the hoardings for information about their duty. Why don't we paste up the ten commandments on all the walls and all the 'buses, and be done with it?"

"Now listen, Miss Watkins," persisted Miss Ford. "I want you to meet Bernard Tovey, the painter, and Ivy MacBee, who founded the Aspiration Club, and Frere, the editor of *I Wonder*, and several other regular Wednesday friends of mine, all interested in the Occult. It would be a real opportunity for you."

"I am afraid you will be very angry with me," said the witch presently in a hollow voice. "If I was occult last night--I'm awfully sorry, but it must have been a fluke. I seem to have said so much last night without knowing it. I'm afraid I was showing off a little."

The painful tears of confession were in her eyes, but she added, changing the subject: "Do you live alone?"

"Yes, absolutely," said Miss Ford. "My friends call me a perfect hermit. I hardly ever have visitors in my spare room, it makes so much work for my three maids."

"I suppose you wouldn't care to divorce your three maids and come and live here," suggested the witch. "I could of course cure you of the nerve-storms you speak of. Or rather I could help you to have nerve-storms all the time, without any stagnant grown-upness in between. Then you wouldn't notice the nerve-storms. This house is a sort of nursing home and college combined. I'll read you the pro-spectus."

*   *   *   *   *

"Very amusing," said Miss Ford, after waiting a minute to see if there was any more of the prospectus. She had quite recovered herself, and was wearing the brisk acute expression that deceived her into claiming a sense of humour. "But why all those uncomfortable rules? And why that discouragement of social intercourse? I am afraid the average person of the class you cater for does not recognise the duty of social intercourse."

"This house," replied the witch, "caters for people who are outside averages. The ferryman says that people who are content to be average are lowering the gen-eral standard. I wish you could have met Peony, the only guest up to now, but she is out, and may be a teeny bit drunk when she comes in. She has gone to draw her money."

"What sort of money?" asked Miss Ford, who was always interested in the sources of income of the Poor.

"Soldier's allotment. Unmarried wife."

The expression of Miss Ford's face tactfully wiped away this bald unfortunate statement from the surface of the conversation. "And how do you make your board-ing-house pay," she asked, "if there is no charge for residence?"

"How d'you mean--pay?" asked the witch. "Pay whom? And what with? Look here, if you will come and live here you shall have a little Wednesday every week on the stairs, under license from me. Harold the Broomstick is apt to shirk clean-ing the stairs, but as it happens, he is keeping company with an O-Cedar Mop in Kentish Town, and I've no doubt she would come over and do the stairs thoroughly every Tuesday night. Besides, we have overalls in stock at only two and eleven three----"

"Oh, I like your merry mood," said Miss Ford, laughing heartily. "You must remember to talk like that when you come to my Wednesdays. Most of my friends are utter Socialists, and believe in bridging as far as possible the gulf between one class and another, so you needn't feel shy or awkward."

The splashing of the ferry-boat was once more heard, and then the shop quaked a little as a heavy foot alighted on the landing-stage. The ferryman was heard saying: "I don't know any party of that name, but I believe the young woman at the shop can help you."

Lady Arabel Higgins entered the shop.

"What, Meta, you here? And Sarah Brown? What a too dretfully funny coincidence. Well, Angela dear, I made a note of your address yesterday, and then lost the note--too dretfully like me. So I rang up the Mayor, and he said he also had made a note, and he would come and show me the way. But I didn't wait for him. I wanted to talk to you about----"

"Well, I must truly be going," interrupted Sarah Brown. "I'll just nip across to the Brown Borough and find a pawn-shop, being hungry."

"There is no need for any one to move on my account," said Lady Arabel. "You all heard what Angela said last night in her little address to the committee in the dark. I don't know why she addressed her remarks particularly at me, but as she did so, there is no secret in the matter. Of course, just at first, it seemed dretful to me that any one should know or speak about it. I cannot understand how you knew, Angela; I am trying not to understand...."

She took up a thin captain biscuit and bit it absent-mindedly. It trembled in her hand like a leaf.

"Yes, it is true that Rrchud isn't like other women's boys. You know it, Meta. Angela evidently knows it, and--at least since yesterday--I know that I know it. His not being able to read or write--I always knew in my heart that my old worn-out tag--'We can't all be literary geniuses'--didn't meet the case. His way of disappearing and never explaining.... Do you know, I have only once seen him with other boys, doing the same as other boys, and that was when I saw him marching with hundreds of real boys ... in 1914.... It was the happiest day I ever had, I thought after all that I had borne a real boy. Well, then, as you know, he couldn't get a commission, couldn't even get his stripe, poor darling. He deserted twice--pure absence of mind--it was always the same from a child--'I wanted to see further,' he'd say, and of course worse in the trenches. Why, you know it all, Angela dear--at least, perhaps not quite all. I should like to tell you--because you said that about the splendour of being the mother of Rrchud....

"Pinehurst--my husband, he is a doctor, you know--had that same passion for seeing further. He was often ill in London. I said it was asthma, but he said it was not being able to see far enough. We were in America for Rrchud's birth, and Pinehurst insisted on going West. I took the precaution of having a good nurse with me. Pinehurst said the East was full of little obstacles, and people's eyes had sucked all the secrets out of the horizon, he said. I like Cape Cod, but he said there was always a wall of sea round those flat wet places. We stayed in a blacksmith's spare room on the desert of Wyoming, but even that horizon seemed a little higher than we, and one clear day, in a pink sunrise, we saw something that might have been a dream, my dears, and might have been the Rockies. Pinehurst couldn't stand that, we pushed west--so tahsome. We climbed a little narrow track up a mountain, in a light buggy that a goldminer lent us. Oh, of course, you'll think us mad, Meta, but, do you know, we actually found the world's edge, a place with no horizon; we looked between ragged pine trees, and saw over the shoulders of great old violet mountains--we saw right down into the stars for ever.... There was a tower of rocks--rose-red rocks in sloping layers--sunny hot by day, my dears, and a great shelter by night. You know, the little dark clouds walk alone upon the mountain tops at sunset--as you said, Angela--they are like trees, and sometimes like faces, and sometimes like the shadows of little bent gipsies.... I used to look at the mountains and think: 'What am I about, to be so worried and so small, in sight of such an enormous storm of mountains under a gold sky?' I think of those rocks often at night, standing just as we left them, all by themselves, under that unnatural moon,--it was an unnatural moon on the edge of the world there,--all by themselves, with no watching eyes to spoil them, as Pinehurst used to say, not even one's own eyes.... You'll say that adventure--my one adventure--was impossible, Meta. Yes, it was. Rrchud was an impossible boy, born on an impossible day, in an impossible place. Ah, my poor Rrchud.... My dears, I am talking dretful nonsense. We were mad. You'd have to know Pinehurst, really, to understand it. Ah, we can never find our mountain again. I can never forgive Pinehurst...."

"You can never repay Pinehurst," said the witch.

Lady Arabel did not seem to hear. For a long time there was nothing to be heard but Sarah Brown, murmuring to her Dog David. You must excuse her, and remember that she lived most utterly alone. She was locked inside herself, and the solitary barred window in her prison wall commanded only a view of the Dog David.

Rrchud's mother said at last: "I really came to tell you that Rrchud came back on leave unexpectedly last night. Of course you must meet him--"

"Rrchud home!" exclaimed Miss Ford. "How odd! I was just telling Miss Watkins about his Power, and how strongly she reminded me of him. Do tell him to keep Wednesday afternoon free."

Lady Arabel, ignoring Miss Ford by mistake, said to the witch: "Will you come on Tuesday to tea or supper?"

"Supper, please," said the witch instantly. Tact, I repeat, was a stranger to her, so she added: "I will bring Sarah Brown too. I bet you twopence she hasn't had a decent meal for days."

And then the Mayor arrived. The witch saw at once that there was some secret understanding between him and her that she did not understand. Her magic escapades often left her in this position. However, she winked back hopefully. But she was not a skilled winker. Everybody--even the Dog David--saw her doing it, and Miss Ford looked a little offended.

CHAPTER III
THE EVERLASTING BOY

Mitten Island is a place of fine weather, its air is always like stained glass between you and perfection. Always you will find in the happy ways of Mitten Island a confidence that the worst is left behind, and that even the worst was not so very bad. You can afford to remember the winter, for even the winter was beautiful; you can smile in the sun and think of the grey flush that used to overspread the island under its urgent crises of snow, and it seems that always there was joy running quickly behind the storms, joy looking with the sun through a tall window in a cloud. Even the most dreadful curtain of a winter's day was always drawn up at sunset; its straight edge rose slowly, disclosing flaming space, and the dramatic figures of the two island churches, exulting and undying martyrs in the midst of flames.

It is a place of fine weather, and this is a book of fine weather, a book written in Spring. I will not remember the winter and the rain. It was the Spring that brought Sarah Brown to Mitten Island, and the Spring that first showed her magic. It was the Spring that awoke her on her first morning in the House of Living Alone.

She awoke because it was so beautiful outside, and because there was a beautiful day coming. You could see the day secretly making preparations behind a shining mist. She heard a sound of breathless singing, and the whipping of stirred grass in the garden, the sound of some one unbearably happy, dancing. Now there is hardly anything but magic abroad before seven o'clock in the morning. Only the disciples of magic like getting their feet wet, and being furiously happy on an empty stomach.

Sarah Brown went to her window. The newborn trembling slants of smoke went up from the houses of the island. There was a sky of that quiet design which suffices half a day unchanged. A garden of quite a good many yards lay behind the house; it contained no potatoes or anything useful, only long, very green grass, and a may tree, and a witch dancing. The extraordinary music to which she was dancing was partly the braying of a neighbouring donkey, and partly her own erratic singing. She danced, as you may imagine, in a very far from grown-up way, rather like a baby that has thought of a new funny way of annoying its Nana; and she sang, too, like a child that inadvertently bursts into loud tuneless song, because it is morning and yet too early to get up. A little wandering of the voice, a little wandering of the feet.... The may tree in the middle of the garden seemed to be her partner. A small blot moved up and down the chequered trunk of the tree, and that was the shadow of a grey squirrel, watching the dancing. The squirrel wore the same fur as the two-and-a-half-guinea young lady wears, and sometimes it looked with a tilted head at the witch, and sometimes it buried its face in its hands and sat for a while shaken with secret laughter. There was certainly something more funny than beautiful about the witch's dancing. She laughed herself most of the time. She was wearing a mackintosh, which was in itself rather funny, but her feet were bare.

A voice broke in: "Good for you, cully."

It was Sarah Brown's fellow-lodger leaning from her window.

The squirrel rippled higher up the may tree.

The pleasure of the thing broke like an eggshell. Sarah Brown turned back towards her bed. It was too early to get up. It was too late to go to sleep again. Eunice, her hot-water bottle, she knew, lay cold as a serpent to shock her feet if she returned. Besides, the Dog David was asleep on the middle of the counterpane, and she was too good a mother to wake him. There are a good many things to do when you find yourself awake too early. It is said that some people sit up and darn their stockings, but I refer now to ordinary people, not to angels. Utterly resourceless people find themselves reduced to reading the penny stamps on yesterday's letters. There is a good deal of food for thought on a penny stamp, but nothing really uplifting. Some people I know employ this morning leisure in scrubbing their consciences clean, thus thriftily making room for the sins of the coming day. But Sarah Brown's conscience was dreadfully receptive, almost magnetic; little sins like smuts lay always deep upon it. There were a few regrettable seconds in every minute she lived, I think, though she never enjoyed the compensations attached to a really considerable sin. Anyway her conscience would have been a case for pumice-stone, and when she was happy she always tried to forget it. Yet she was not without a good many very small and unessential resources for sleepless moments. Often she wrote vague comments on matters with which she was not familiar, in an exercise-book, always eventually mislaid. She would awake from dear and unspeakable dreams full of hope, and tell herself stories about herself, trying on various lives and deaths like clothes. The result was never likely enough even to laugh at.

To-day she had watched magic dancing in a mackintosh, and she was at a loss.

There was a knock upon her door, and a voice: "Hi, cocky, could you oblige me with a loan of a few 'alfpence for the milkman. I 'aven't a bean in me purse."

"Nor have I," said Sarah Brown, opening the door. "But I can pawn--"

"Ow, come awf it, Cuffbut," said the fellow-lodger. "This is a respectable 'ouse, more or less, and you ain't goin' out to pawn nothink in your py-jams. I'll owe it to the milkman again. Not but what I 'adn't p'raps better pay 'im after all. I got me money paid yesterday, on'y I 'ad thought to put it away for Elbert."

"Are you Peony, the other lodger?"

"Thet's right, dearie."

Peony was not in her first youth, in fact she was comfortably into her second. Her voice was so beautiful that it almost made one shy, but her choice of language, tending as it did in the other direction, reassured one. She had fine eyes of an absolute grey, and dark hair parted in the middle and drawn down so as to make a triangle of a face which, left to itself, would have been square. Her teeth spoilt her; the gaps among them looked like the front row of the stalls during the first scene of a revue, or the last scene of a play by Shakspere. On the whole, she looked like the duckling of the story, serenely conscious of a secret swanhood. She showed unnatural energy even in repose, and lived as though she had a taxi waiting at the door.

"Who's Elbert?" asked Sarah Brown, and then wished she had not asked, for even without Peony's flush she should have guessed.

"'Arf a mo, kiddie, till I get rid of the milkman. Come an' sit on the stairs, an' I'll tell you a tale. I like no end tellin' this tale."

Harold the Broomstick was desultorily sweeping the stairs. He worked harder when first conscious of being watched, but seeing that they intended to stay there, on the top step, he made this the excuse to disappear indolently, leaving little heaps of dust on several of the lower steps.

"I come across Elbert first when I was about eight an' twenty," said Peony, when Sarah Brown, in rather a loud dressing-gown, had taken her seat on the stairs beside her. "Elbert was the ideel kid, an' me--nothing to speak of. Nothin' more than a lump o' mud, I use to say. All my life, if you'll believe me, cully, I've lived in mud--an' kep' me eye on the moon, so to say. I worked in a factory all day, makin' mud, as it were, for muddy Jews, an' every Saturday night I took 'ome twelve shillin's-worth o' mud to keep meself alive in a city o' mud until the Saturday after. But o' nights there was the moon, or else the stars, or else the sunset, an' anyway all the air between to look at. I 'ad a back room, 'igh up, and o' nights I use to sit an' breave there, an' look at the sky. Believe me, dearie, I was mad about breavin'--it was me only recreation, so to say. By Gawd, it's a fair wonder 'ow the sky an' the air keeps on above the mud, and 'ow we looks at it, an' breaves it, an' never pays no rent for it, when all's said an' done. There ain't never a penny put in the slot for the moonlight, when you come to think of it, yet still it all goes on. Well, in those days, I never spoke to a soul, an' 'ated everybody, an' I got very queer, queerer nor many as is locked up in Claybury this minute. I got to thinkin' as 'ow there was a debt 'anging over us all, some'ow the sky seemed like a sort of upper floor to all our 'ouses, with the stars an' the moon for windows, an' it seemed like as if there did oughter be some rent to pay, though the Landlord was a reel gent and never pressed for it. There might be people 'oo lived among flowers in the sunlight, an', so to say, rented the parlour floor, but not me. I 'ad the upper floor, an' breaved the light o' the moon. As for flowers--bless you, I'd never 'ardly seen a flower stuck proper to the ground until a year ago. Well, dearie, I use to make believe as 'ow we'd all get a charnce, all to ourselves, to pay what we owed. Some people, I thought, runs away from the debt, an' some pays it in bad money, but, I ses to meself, if ever my charnce come, I'll pay it the very best I can. Lawd, 'ow I 'ated everybody in those days. It seemed like people was all rotten, an' as if all the churches an' all the cherities was the rottenest of all the lot. Well, then, dearie, Elbert blew in. You know what kids is mostly like in the Brown Borough, but Elbert--'e never was. Straight legs 'e 'ad, an' never a chilblain nor a sore, an' a small up-lookin' face, an' yallery 'air--what you could see of it, for of course I always made 'im keep it nicely cropped to the pink. You never see sich a clean boy, you never see 'im but what 'e seemed to 'ave sponged 'is collar that minute, an' the little seat to 'is breeks always patched in the right colour, an' all. Yet 'e wasn't one of them choir-boy kinds, 'e could 'ave 'is little game with the best of 'em, an' often kicked up no end of a row when we was playin' pretendin' games of a wet Sunday. 'E 'ad one little game 'e loved best of all--not marbles, it wasn't, nor peg-tops--but there, I won't tell you what it was, for you'd laugh like the gal at the shop did when I spoke of it. I don't often get talkin', but I'd 'ad a nip of brandy at the time. Laugh fit to bust, she did--'avin' 'ad a nip of the same 'erself--an' as't if Elbert wasn't blind as well, an' if 'e wore any clothes besides wings.... The funny thing was thet Elbert did 'ave bad sight, it always seemed odd to me thet with 'is weak eyes 'e should choose to play the little game 'e did. I use to take 'im to the 'Eath of a summer Sunday, an' 'e use to stand on them little ridges below the Spaniards Road, with 'is eyes shut against the sun, never botherin' to take no aim. I can see 'im now, a-pulling of the string of 'is bow--it 'ad an 'igh note, like the beginnin' of a bit o' music--an' then awf 'e'd go like a rebbit, to see where the arrer fell. It was always a marvel to me 'e didn't put somebody's eye out, but I didn't mind--I 'ated everybody. 'E didn't live with me, 'e just came in an' out. 'E never tol' me 'is name was Elbert--I just called 'im thet, the prettiest name I knew. 'E never tol' me 'oo 'is people were; I shouldn't think they could 'ave bin Brown Borough people, for Elbert seemed to 'ave bin about a lot, seen mountains an' oceans an' sich-like, an' come acrost a lot of furriners--even Germans. 'E talked a lot about people--as good as a novelette 'is stories was, but bloody 'igh-flavoured. Children knows a lot in the Brown Borough. 'Ow 'e'd noticed the things 'e 'ad with them blindish eyes of 'is, I don't know. I got to count on that boy no end. Fair drunk with satisfaction, I use to feel. Call me a fool if you like, cully, but it was three or four year before I got the idee that there was anythink funny about Elbert. It was when it begun to look as if the War 'ad come to stop, an' one couldn't look at any boy without countin' up to see 'ow long 'e 'ad before the Army copped 'im. An' then I calc'lated that Elbert should be rising fourteen now, an' I saw then thet 'e 'adn't grown an inch since I first see 'im, nor 'e hadn't changed 'is ways, but still 'e run about laughin', playin' 'is little kiddy-game, with 'is face to the sun. An' then I remembered 'ow often 'e'd tol' me things thet seemed too 'istorical for sich as 'im to come by honest, tales about blokes in 'istory--nanecdotes 'e'd use to pass acrost about Admiral Nelson, or Queen Bess--she use to make 'im chuckle, she did--an' a chap called Shilly or Shally, 'oo was drownded. An' I got struck all of an 'eap, to think 'e was some sort of an ever-lasting boy, an' p'raps 'e was a devil, I thought, an' p'raps I'd sold me soul without knowin' it. I never took much stock of me soul, but I always 'ad that debt o' mine in me mind, an' I wanted to pay it clean. For them London mists agin the sky in the Spring, an' for the moonlight, an' for the sky just before a thunderstorm--all them things seemed to 'ave come out of the same box, like, an' I didn't like feelin' as 'ow they was all jest charity.... 'Owever, I got this idee about Elbert, an' I didn't sleep a wink thet night, an' couldn't enjoy me starlight. In the mornin' 'e come as usual, with 'is pretty blind smile, an' I ses to 'im: 'Elbert,' I ses, 'You ain't a crool boy, are you? You wouldn't do anythink to 'urt me?' Lookin' at 'im, I couldn't believe it. ''Urt you?' 'e ses quite 'appily; 'an' why wouldn't I 'urt you? I'd as lief send you to the Devil as not,' 'e ses. Well, cocky, I don't mind tellin' you I lost me 'ead at that. I run awiy--run awiy from my Elbert--Oh, Gosh! I bin an' give up me bits o' sticks to a neighbour, an' got a place, an' went into service. I sneaked out one night, when Elbert 'ad gone 'ome. I got a place up Kilburn way, an ol' couple, retired from the pawnbrokin' line. The ol' man 'ad softening in 'is brain, an' said one thing all the blessed time, murmurin' like a bee. The ol' woman never spoke, never did no work, lef' it all to me. She was always a-readin' of 'er postcard album, shiftin' the cards about--she 'ad thousands, besides one 'ole book full of seaside comics. A beautiful collection. Well, I was dishin' up the tea one night in the kitchen, an' I 'eard a laugh--Elbert's laugh, like three little bells--an' there was Elbert lookin' in at the window. I run after 'im--there wasn't nobody there. When I come back the tripe was burnt an' I lef' it on the fire an' run away, thet minute. They owed me wages, but I didn't stop for nothink. I was frightened. I got a place afterwards up Islington, three ol' sisters, kep' a fancy shop, fought with each other every minute of their lives. I 'adn't bin there two days before Elbert walked in, jest as laughin' an' lovin' as ever. I see then it was no use, good or bad 'e'd got me. I let 'im sit in my kitchen, an' give 'im some sugar-bread. An' one of the ol' cat-sisters come in. ''Oo's this?' she ses. 'A young friend o' mine,' I ses. 'You're a liar,' she ses, 'I seed from the first min-ute as you wasn't no respectable gal,' she ses, 'an' now per'aps me sisters'll believe me. So out I 'ad to go, an' I wasn't sorry. It seemed like there wasn't nothink in the world mattered but Elbert, like as if damnation was worth while. 'Ow, Elbert,' I ses, 'I'd go to the Devil for you, an' smile all the way.' 'E laughed an' laughed. 'Come on,' 'e ses, 'to-day's an 'oliday.' Though it wasn't, it was a Tuesday in August. 'Come on,' 'e ses, 'get yer best 'at on,' an' 'e gives me a yaller rose, for me button-'ole. A year ago come August, thet was. I follered Elbert at a run all up the City Road, an' near the Angel we took a taxi. 'Tell 'im Euston Station,' ses Elbert, an' so I did. You know the 'uge top o' thet station from the 'ill by the Angel--well, kid, I tell you I saw a reel mountain for the first time, when I saw thet. It was the 'eat mist, an' a sort o' pink light made a reel 'ighland landscape out of it. I paid the taxi-man over 'alf of all the money I 'ad, an' we went to the ticket-awfice. 'Elbert,' I ses, 'where shell we book to,' I ses, like that, though I 'adn't 'ardly a bloody oat in me purse. 'Take a platform ticket,' 'e ses, an' so I did. But 'e run on to the platform without no ticket, an' begun dancin' up an' down among the people like a mad thing, but nobody seemed to mind 'im. I set down on a seat to watch 'im. I thought: 'Blimey,' I thought, 'if I ain't under thet blinkin' mountain now, an' all these people,' I ses, 'is the Little People they tell of, that lives inside 'ills, an' on'y comes out under the moon.' I remembered thet moonlight debt o' mine, an' I thought--'I'm done with the mud now, I'm comin' alive now,' I ses, 'and this'll be my charnce.' Presently Elbert come back to me, an' 'e was draggin' a soldier by the 'and. 'This is a magic man,' ses Elbert, 'come back from livin' under the sky. Can't you feel the magic?' 'e ses.

"Well, dearie, take it 'ow you will, thet's 'ow I met my Sherrie. A magic man 'e was, for 'e 'ad my ticket taken, an' never seemed surprised. Ten days leave 'e 'ad, an' we spent it at an inn in a village on a moor, jest a mile out o' sound of the sea. The moor an' the sea, touchin' each other. ... Oh Gawd!... The sea was like my sky at night come nearer--come near enough to know better, like. In between the moor an' the sea there was the beach--it looked like a blessed boundary road between two countries, an' it led away to where you couldn't see nothing more except a little white town, sort of built 'igh upon a mist, more like a star.... Oh Gawd!...

"Anyway, Cuffbut, thet was me charnce, an' thet's 'ow I come to know 'ow my debt was goin' to be paid. Sherrie understood all thet. 'E was a magic man, 'e was. At least, 'e was mostly magic, but some of 'im was nothin' but a fool when all's said an' done--like any other man. I couldn't 'ave done with an all-magic bloke. Ow, 'e was a fool.... All the things 'e might 'ave bin able to do, like polishin' 'is equipment, or findin' 'is clean socks, 'e use to forever be askin' me to do. I loved doin' it. But all the things 'e couldn't do at all, like drawin' me likeness, or cuttin' out a blouse for me, 'e was forever tryin' to do."

She spoke of Sherrie as a naturalist would speak of a new animal, gradually finding out the pretty and amusing ways of the creature.

"I called 'im Sherrie because thet's what 'e called me. A French word it was, 'e ses, meaning 'dearie,' as it were. 'E was a reel gent, was Sherrie. I as't 'im once why 'e took up with a woman like me, instead of with a reel young lady. 'E ses as 'ow 'e'd never met before anybody 'oo seed themselves from outside an' yet was fairly honest. I know what 'e meant, for I was always more two people than one, an' I watch meself sometimes as if I was a play. I wouldn't be tellin' you this story, else. Well, dearie, Elbert was always in an' out, an' always a-hollerin' an' a-laughin' an' a-playin' 'is game. 'E stayed with us all them ten days, an' 'e come with me to Victoria, to see Sherrie off to France. It's Sherrie's allotted money what I fetch every week. But I won't touch it, I puts it away for Elbert. I don't want to owe nothin' to nobody, for I'm payin' sich a big debt. Elbert, when 'e comes back to me, 'e's going to be my payment to the world, an' it's got to be good money. For Elbert left me after Sherrie went. 'E said as 'ow 'e was going 'ome, an' as 'ow 'e would come back to me in the Spring, an' stay with me always. It wasn't like partin', e' ses, 'im an' me could never do thet. I know what 'e meant, now...."

"And what about Sherrie?" asked Sarah Brown.

"Oh, Sherrie, 'e never writes to me. But 'e promised too to come back in the Spring, an' so 'e will, for there ain't no Boche bullet that can 'it a magic man."

"It's springtime now," said Sarah Brown.

"It's springtime now," repeated Peony. "Ow, it's wonderful, seems like as if I was gettin' too much given me, so as I can never repay. But I'm keepin' count, I'm not forgettin'. It ain't long now before I'll pay my debt. Come the middle o' May...."

CHAPTER IV
THE FORBIDDEN SANDWICH

While Sarah Brown's unenviable leisure was spent in acting as slave to committees, she had at the same time a half-time profession which, when she was well enough to follow it, brought twenty shillings a week to her pocket. She was in the habit of sitting every morning in a small office, collecting evidence from charitable spies about the Naughty Poor, and, after wrapping the evidence in mysterious ciphers, writing it down very beautifully upon little cards, so that the next spy might have the benefit of all his forerunners' experience. Sarah Brown never thought about the theory of this work, because the different coloured inks and the beautiful writing pleased her so.

There are people to whom a ream of virgin paper is an inspiration, who find the first sharpening of a pencil the most lovable of all labours, who see something almost holy in the dedication of green and red penholders to their appropriate inks, in whose ears and before whose eyes the alphabet is like a poem or a prayer. Touch on stationery and you touched an insane spot in Sarah Brown's mind. Her dream of a perfect old age was staged in a stationer's shop in a quiet brown street; there she would spend twilit days in stroking thick blotting-paper, in drawing dogs--all looking one way--with new pen-nibs, in giving advice in a hushed voice to connoisseur customers, who should come to buy a diary or a book-plate or a fountain-pen with the same reverence as they now show who come to buy old wine.

Therefore Sarah Brown's hand had found ideal employment on a charity register. As for her mind, it usually shut its eye during office hours. Her Dog David liked the work too, as the hearth-rug was a comfortable one, and Charity, though it may suffer long in other directions, is rather particular about its firing.

On the Monday after her change of home, Sarah Brown found that the glory had gone out of the varied inks, and even a new consignment of index-cards, exquisitely unspotted from the world, failed to arouse her enthusiasm. This was partly because the first name in the index that she looked up was that of Watkins, Thelma Bennett, single, machinist. The ciphers informed the initiated that Watkins had called on the War Association, to ask for Help and Advice, See Full Report. Sarah Brown felt sad and clumsy, and made two blots, one in green on the Watkins card, and the other in ordinary Stephens-colour on the card of one Tonk, chocolate-box-maker, single, to whom a certain charity was obstinately giving a half-pint of milk daily, regardless of the fact that last month she had received a shilling's-worth of groceries from the Parish.

The air of that office rang with the name of Tonk that morning. Hardly had the industrious Sarah Brown finished turning the blot upon her card into the silhouette of a dromedary by a few ingenious strokes of the pen, when the lady representing the obstinate charity came in, her lips shaped to the word Tonk.

"Tonk," she said. "Late of Mud Street. She has changed her address. I am the Guild of Happy Hearts. She still comes to fetch her half-pint of milk daily, and only yesterday I learnt from a neighbour that she had left Mud Street three weeks ago. It really is disgraceful the way these poor people conceal important facts from us. Have you her new address?"

"Our last address for Tonk was 12 Mud Street," answered Sarah Brown coldly. "But we have already notified you three times that the woman is not entitled to milk from the Happy Hearts, as she has been having parish relief, as well as an allotment."

"Tonk is--hm--hm," said the Happy Heart delicately in an undertone, so that the blushing masculine ear of the Dog David might be spared. "After Baby Week, you know, we feel bound to help all hm--hm women as far as we can, regardless of other considerations--"

"Really you oughtn't to. Tonk is posing as a single chocolate-box-maker." Sarah Brown was rapidly becoming exasperated with everybody concerned, but not least with the evidently camouflaging Tonk.

"She has a soldier at the Front," said the Happy Heart. "I am sorry to say that she will not promise to marry him, even if he does come home. But even so--"

Sarah Brown wrote down on Miss Tonk's card the small purple cipher that stood for hm--hm. "I will make enquiries about her address," she said.

But that was not the last of Tonk. Presently the red face of the Relieving Officer loomed over the index.

"In the case of Plummett--" he began loudly.

"In the case of Tonk--" interrupted Sarah Brown, to whom, in her present mood, Plummett could only have been a last straw. She hated the Relieving Officer unjustly, because he knew she was deaf and raised his voice, with the best intentions, to such a degree that the case papers on the index were occasionally blown away. "We have already notified you three times that Tonk is having a half-pint of milk daily from the Happy Hearts, as well as an allotment from a soldier."

"We stopped the groceries," roared the Relieving Officer. "But in the case of Plummett--"

"In the case of Tonk--" persisted Sarah Brown. "She has moved from Mud Street, can you tell me her last address?"

"She is living in a sort of private charitable institution, somewhere on the outskirts of the district--Mitten Island, I fancy. I don't know the exact address, because we have stopped the groceries, she paying no rent now. In the case of Plummett, I thought you might be interested to know that she got a month this morning for assaulting the Sanitary Inspector--pulling his nose, I hear. She told the magistrate it struck her as being a useless nose if it didn't notice anything wrong with her drains. The children came into the House this morning."

"What is Tonk's Christian name?" asked Sarah Brown, who had been a changed woman since Mitten Island was mentioned.

"I forget. Some flower name, I think. Probably Lily or Ivy. In the case of M'Clubbin, the woman is said to have fallen through a hole in the floor of the room she and her three children slept in. She was admitted into the Infirmary last night, and her furniture will be sold to pay her rent--"

"It begins with P," said Sarah Brown. "P. Tonk, unmarried wife, of Mitten Island...."

The Relieving Officer went away, for it was dinner-time. Sarah Brown absently unwrapped the little dinner which she had brought hanging by a thin string from a strangled finger. Mustard sandwiches with just a flavouring of ham, and a painfully orthodox 1918-model bun, made of stubble. Sarah Brown almost always forgot the necessity of food until she was irrevocably in the 'bus on her way to work. But this morning, as she had taken her seat with David in the bouncing ferry-boat, there had been a panting rustling noise behind her, and Harold the Broomstick had swept a little packet of sandwiches into her lap. He had disappeared before she had been able to do more than turn over in her mind the question whether or no broomsticks ever expect to be tipped.

Now I could not say with certainty whether the witch, in making up this packet of sandwiches, had included the contents of one of her own little packets of magic. Sarah Brown would have been very susceptible to such a drug; her mind was always on the brink of innocent intoxication. Perhaps she was only half a woman, so that half a joy could make her heart reel and sing, and half a sorrow break it. She was defenceless against impressions, and too many impressions make the heart very tired. Therefore, I think, she was a predestined victim of magic, and it seems unlikely that the witch should have missed such an opportunity to dispense spells.

After the first bite at the first sandwich, Sarah Brown was conscious of a Joke somewhere. This feeling in itself was akin to delirium, for there are no two facts so remote as a Joke and a Charity Society. The office table confronted Sarah Brown, and she wondered that she could ever have seen it as anything but a butt. She wondered how she had been able to sit daily in front of that stout and earnest index without poking it in the ribs and making a fool of it. The office clock, alone among clocks, had never played a practical joke. The sad fire below it, conscious of a Mission, was overloaded with coal and responsibility.

The second bite, ten minutes later, caused Sarah Brown to be tired and distrustful of a room that had no smile. Her eyes turned to seek the hidden Joke beyond the limits of that lamentable room. There was a spring-coloured tree in the school-ground opposite, and above the tree a rough blue and silver sky contradicted all the doctrines preached in offices. There was in the wind something of the old raw simplicity and mirth that always haunts the sea, and penetrates inland only on rare spring days. The high white clouds crossed the sky like galleons, like old stories out of the innocent Eden-like past of the sea, before she learnt the ways of steam and secret killing. Old names of ships came to Sarah Brown's mind ... Castle-of-Comfort ... Cloud-i'-the-Sun....

"I am doing wrong," said Sarah Brown. She took a third bite.

And then she felt the spirit of the Naughty Poor in the room; there was laughter, as of the registered, in the ears of the Registrar. It is not really permissible for the Naughty Poor to invade offices which exist to do them good. The way of charity lies through suspicion, but the suspicion of course must be all on one side. We have to judge the criminal unheard; if we called him as a witness in his case we might become sentimental. The Charity Society may be imagined as keeping two lists of crimes, a short one for Registrars and Workers, and a very long one for the registered. High on the list of crimes possible to Registrars and Workers is Sentimentality. It is sentimental to feel personal affection for a Case, or to give a child of the Naughty Poor a penny without full enquiry, or to say "A-goo" to a grey pensive baby eating dirt on the pavement, or to acknowledge the right of a Case to ask questions sometimes instead of answering them, or to disapprove of spying and tale-bearing, or to believe any statement made by any one without an assured income, or to quote any part of the New Testament, or in fact to confuse in any way the ideas of charity and love. Christ, who, by the way, unfortunately omitted to join any reputable philanthropic society, commanded seekers of salvation to be poor and to despise themselves. But this was sentimental, and the Charity Society decrees that only the prosperous and the self-respectful shall deserve a hearing.

"I am sentimental," said Sarah Brown to her Dog David in a broken voice. She turned again to her enchanted sandwich.

There was increased laughter in the air, and through it she heard the hoarse and happy shouting of the sparrows in the spring-coloured tree opposite. Sparrows are the ideal Naughty Poor, the begging friars, the gypsies of the air, they claim alms as a right and as a seal of friendship; with their mouths full of your crumbs they share with you their innocent and vulgar wit, they give you in return no I.O.U., and no particulars for your case-paper. When they have got from you all that you will give, they wink and giggle and shake the dust of your window-sill from off their feet.

Sarah Brown opened the office window, and the air of the office began at once to dance with life and the noise of children and birds. She thought perhaps these were magic noises, for she heard them so clearly. She broke her second sandwich upon the window-sill, and the sparrows crossed the street and stood on the area railing in a row below her, all speaking at once in an effort to convey to her the fact that a retreat on her part would be tactful.

The sparrow obviously buys all his clothes ready-made, probably at Jumble Sales, and he always seems to choose clothes made for a stouter bird. There is no reason why he should never look chic; he has a slimmer figure than the bullfinch, for instance, who always manages to look so well-tailored. It is just arrogance, pure Londonism, on the part of the sparrow, just that impudent socialistic spirit that makes it so difficult for us to reform the Naughty Poor.

Sarah Brown retreated one step. "I'm not going farther away. Either you eat that sandwich with me looking on, or you leave it."

The sparrows whispered together for a moment, saying to each other, "You go first." They obviously knew that it was a charity window-sill, and were afraid Sarah Brown might intend to rebuke them for not shutting their beaks while chewing, or for neglecting to put any crumbs into the Savings Bank. But after a minute one sparrow moistened his beak and came.... He ate, they all ate, and did not seek to escape as the door of the office opened and the witch came in. She went straight to the window and picked up from among the stooping sparrows a piece of the broken sandwich, and ate it. The Dog David was making sure that there was no surviving crumb on the floor to tell the tale of his mother's sentimental weakness. Almost instantly, therefore, that sandwich was but a memory, a fading taste in about twenty beaks and two mouths. But still the window stood open, and the air danced, and the white reflections of the ship-like clouds lay on the oilcloth floor.

Sarah Brown in the meanwhile, disregarding the witch, had returned to the index, and had taken from its drawer a notification form. In the space given for Name of Case she had written in her irreproachable printing hand:

"CHARITY, Cautionary Case, 12 Pan Street, Brown Borough. With reference to the above case, I have to report that it seems unsatisfactory. There are indeed grave suspicions that the above name is only an alias, the address being also probably false, for the genuine Charity's place of origin is said to be the home rather than the office. The present registrar is at a loss to identify with certainty this case. It would seem to be one of the Habits that haunt the world, collecting Kudos under assumed names...."

"It puzzles me," said the witch, looking out of the window, "why one never sees two birds collide. If there were as many witches in the air as there are birds, I bet you twopence there would be constant accidents. Do you think they have any sort of a rule of the road, or do they indicate with their beaks--"

"Witch," said Sarah Brown, "I have got to say something."

"Oh, have you?" said the witch, a little disappointed at being interrupted. "Oh, well, I can sympathise, I know what that feels like. Get on and say it."

The Dog David, who was really a good and attentive son to Sarah Brown, came and laid his chin, with an exaggerated look of interest, on her knee-cap.

"Is it any use," said Sarah Brown, "fighting against the Habits in the world, there are so many. Who set these strange and senseless deceivers at large? Religion which has forgotten ecstasy.... Law which has forgotten justice.... Charity which has forgotten love.... Surely magic has suffered at the stake for saner ideals than these?"

"Why, of course," said the witch impatiently. "Magic generally suffered *because* it was so sane. I thought everybody knew that."

"All habits. All habits," chanted Sarah Brown. "What is this Charity, this clinking of money between strangers, and when did Charity cease to be a comforting and secret thing between one friend and another? Does Love make her voice heard through a committee, does Love employ an almoner to convey her message to her neighbour?"

"Not that I know of," sighed the witch. "Sarah Brown, how long do you want me to keep quiet, while you say things that everybody surely knows?"

But Sarah Brown went on. "The real Love knows her neighbour face to face, and laughs with him and weeps with him, and eats and drinks with him, so that at last, when his black day dawns, she may share with him, not what she can spare, but all that she has."

The Dog David grunted a little, by way of rather dubious applause. Sarah Brown, with her own voice printed loud and stark upon the retina of her hearing, felt a little abashed. But presently she added in a whisper: "Listen. I am a spy. I am a lover of specially recommended neighbours only. I am here to help to give the black cloud Tyranny a rather dirty silver lining. I am the False Steward, in the interest of the Superfluously Comfortable. My Masters sit upon the King's Highway, taking toll in bitterness and humiliation from every traveller along that road. For surely comfort is every man's heritage, surely the happy years should come to every man--not doled out, not meanly dependent on his moral orthodoxy, but as his right. The fat philanthropist is a debtor, but he behaves like a creditor; he distributes obliga-tions with his gold, yet he has no right to the gold he gives. He makes his brother beg upon his knees for the life and the health and the dear opportunity that should have been that brother's birthright."

"You are possessed, dear Sarah Brown," said the witch. "Don't be frightened, it will soon pass off. I knew a girl who had an attack very much like this; while she was under its influence she made up a psalm pretty nearly as good as one of David's. Her mother was much alarmed about her. But she recovered quite quickly, except that she left her job as typist in a mind-improving institute and went to sea as a stewardess."

Sarah Brown talked on, louder and louder. "Too long I have been a servant in the house of this stranger, this greedy Charity; too long have I sat--a silly proxy for the Too-Fortunate--in this narrow stiff-backed judgement-seat from ten till three daily. There is Love and April outside the window, there is too much wind and laughter outside to allow of the forming of Habits. I have seen Love and the Spring only through the glass of a charity office window, the rude voices of children and sparrows and other inheritors of opportunity have been dulled for me by grey panes. The white ships ... Castle-of-Comfort ... Cloud-i'-the-Sun have sailed into port from the open sky without a cargo for me...."

"Good God!" said Sarah Brown, pushing David from her. "What has happened to me? I have become sentimental."

The room seemed to her wild imagination to be full of the spirits of parsons and social workers with flaming swords, pointing at the door.

"Well, that's the end of that job," said the witch. "I'll tell you what, let's go and sit on the Swing-leg Seat on the Heath. The air there and the look of Harrow church steeple'll do you good."

"I am damned. I am a Cautionary Case," cried Sarah Brown, and she slunk behind the witch through the frowning gate of her Eden of fair inks and smooth white surfaces. She had shared with David the remains of her Sandwich of Knowl-edge; she had left on the table her puny paper defiance. David, except that he had required but little temptation, had played Adam's part very creditably in the affair. For him Eden had been a soft warm place, and he was anxious to blame somebody--the woman for choice--for the loss of his comfort. He followed her out into the cold, to become, as you shall hear, like Adam, a tiller of the soil.

CHAPTER V
AN AIR RAID SEEN FROM BELOW

Magic is a disconcerting travelling companion. While seldom actually conspicuous, it seems to have a mysterious and varying effect on the surrounding public. I have met travellers by Tube who tell of strange doings in those regions, when the conductor of one compartment fell suddenly in love with the conductress of the next, and they ran to each other and met in the middle of the car. As nobody opened the gates or rang the bells, the bewildered train stood for hours at Mornington Crescent before any member of the watching public could find the heart to interrupt the pretty scene. It is patent that a magic person must have been the more or less deliberate cause of this episode. Then again, there is the story of the 'bus that went mad, just as it was leaving its burrow at Dalston. It got the idea that the kindly public was its enemy. You should have seen the astonishment of Liverpool Street and the Bank as it rushed by them. Old ladies about to ask it whether it went to Clapham--its label said it was bound for Barnes--stood aghast, and their questions died on their lips. Policemen put up their hands against it,--it ran over them. It even learned the trick of avoiding the nimble business man by a cunning little skid just as he thought he had caught it. You will hardly believe me, but that 'bus ran seven times round Trafalgar Square, until the lions' tails twisted for giddiness, and Nelson reeled where he stood. I don't know where it went to that day, certainly not to Barnes, but late in the evening it burst into another 'bus's burrow at Tooting, its sides heaving, its tyres worn to the quick, its windows streaming with perspiration, and a great bruise on its forehead where a chance bomb had struck it. I believe the poor thing had to be put out of its misery in the end. And what was the reason of all this? It was found that a wizard, called Innocent, of Stoke Newington, had been asleep on the top all the time, having forgotten to alight the night before, on his return from the City.

Sarah Brown, on the night of Lady Arabel's supper party, was unaware of the risk she ran in entering a public conveyance in company with a witch. But she was spared to a merciful extent, for nothing happened on any of the 'buses they boarded, except that, as they crossed the Canal, a cloud of sea-gulls swooped and swirled into the 'bus, resting awhile on the passengers' willing shoulders before disappearing again. Also the passengers on the Baker Street stretch sang part-songs, all the way down to Selfridge's. The conductor turned out to have rather a pleasing tenor voice.

The witch and Sarah Brown knocked at the Higgins' door five minutes before supper-time. Lady Arabel herself opened it.

"My dears, isn't it too dretful. All our servants are gone. It's an extraordinary thing, they never can stand Rrchud and his ways."

The tactful Sarah Brown nudged the witch. "Better not stay," she murmured.

"Of course we'll stay," replied the witch loudly. "I'm horribly hungry, and there's sure to be some supper."

"Certainly there is," added Lady Arabel. "I cooked it myself. Do you know, I've never seen a cookery book before, and the little pictures of animals with the names of joints written all over them shocked me dretfully. I feel I could have a too deliciously intimate conversation with a bullock now."

The house of Higgins had an enormous hall to which a large number of high windows gave the impression of a squint. I should think two small Zeppelins could have danced a minuet under its dome. Sarah Brown and the witch put on their cathedral look at once, by mistake, and propping their chins upon their umbrellas gazed reverently upward.

"Too dretful, a house of this size without servants," said Lady Arabel. "The fourth footman was the last to go. He said even the Army would be better than this. He liked spooks, he said, at second hand, but not otherwise. Too funny how people take dear Rrchud seriously. I'm glad to say the orchestra has stayed with us. Come into Rrchud's study, won't you, while I just go and help the first violin to dish up the soup."

Sarah Brown and the witch were left in a small room that opened on to the great hall. It was furnished rather like a lodging-house parlour. There was a thermometer elaborately disguised as a model of the Eddystone Lighthouse on the mantelpiece, flanked on each side by a china boot in pink, with real bootlaces, and a pig looking out of the top of each. There were pictures on the walls, mostly representing young ladies, more or less obviously in love, supported by rustic properties. I have noticed that the girl's first love is the monopoly of the Victorian painter, whereas the boy's is that of the novelist, but I do not know the reason of this.

There was a slight clap of thunder and Richard entered. He would have been very obviously a wizard even without the thunder, and seemed much less innocent about his magic than the witch. He had pale hair, a pale face, and eyes that did not open wide without a certain effort on the part of the brows.

"You are despising my ornaments," he said to Sarah Brown. "I admire them awfully. I don't like really clever art. Do you know, it makes me sneeze."

Directly he spoke, one saw that he was making the usual effort of magic to appear real. Witches and wizards lead difficult lives because they have no ancestry working within them to prompt them in the little details. Whenever you see a person being unusually grown-up, suspect them of magic. You can always notice witches and wizards, for instance, after eight o'clock at night, pretending that they are not proud of sitting up late. It is all nonsense about witches being night birds; they often fly about at night, indeed, but only because they are like permanent children gloriously escaped for ever from their Nanas.

"This picture," added Richard, "seems to me very beautiful." The picture might have cost a shilling originally, framed, or it might have been attached to a calendar once. It was a landscape so thick in colouring and so lightless that it failed to give an outdoor impression at all. There was a river and waterfall like well-combed hair in the middle, and a dozen leaden mountains lying about with--apparently--pocket-handkerchiefs on their tops, and a dropsical-looking stag drinking. "I can't imagine," insisted Richard, "that there could be a more beautiful picture than that, but perhaps it appeals to me specially because father and mother and I so often talk about the place together--the place like that, near to the mountain where I was born. That was in the Rockies, you know, and just below our mountain I am sure there was a canyon like that--I dream of it--with milky-green water running under and over and round the most extraordinary shapes of ice, and cactuses like green hedgehogs in the crevices of the rocks, and great untidy pine-trees clinging to an ounce of earth on an inch of flat surface. And the rocks are a most splendid rose-red, and lie in steep layers, and break out into shapes that are so deliberate, they look as if they must mean something. Indeed they do...."

A stave played by a 'cello called them to supper, and, as they returned to the hall, a burst of earnest music from the whole orchestra partially drowned the clap of thunder that again marked Richard's passage through the door. Sarah Brown felt sure that Lady Arabel arranged this on purpose. The wizard's mother obviously had great difficulty in not noticing the phenomena connected with her son, and she wore a striving smile and a look of glassy and well-bred unconsciousness whenever anything magic happened.

At the end of the hall the orchestra, arranged neatly in a crescent, was busily employing its violins in a unanimous melody of so rude and destructive a nature that it seemed as if every string must be broken. This mania spread until even the outlying bassoons, triangles, and celestas were infected. A piercing note of command, however, from a clarinet caused a devastating dumbness to fall suddenly on every instrument except the piano, which continued self-consciously alone. The pianist looked at the ceiling mostly, but one note seemed to be an especial favourite with him, and whenever he played it he looked closely and paternally at it, almost indeed applying his nose to it. All at once, just as Sarah Brown was beginning to imagine that she could catch the tune and the time, the music ceased, apparently in the middle of a bar. Richard sneezed once or twice. That unsophisticated wizard was evidently enjoying himself in the practice of his art. One felt that magic was not encouraged in the Army, and that the supernatural orgy in which he was now indulging was the accumulated reaction after long self-control. Strange noises of unnatural laughter, for instance, proceeded from distant corners of the hall, and each of the electric lights in turn winked facetiously. The string of the double bass broke loudly, and the new string which its devotee laboriously inserted also broke at once. The performer looked appealingly at Lady Arabel, but she refrained from meeting his eye. A blizzard of butterflies enveloped the table. This was evidently rather a difficult trick, for the spell collapsed repeatedly, and from one second to another Sarah Brown was never quite sure whether there were really Purple Admirals drowning in her soup or not.

"You are so lucky," sighed the witch, "plenty of room and every facility. I myself am so dreadfully cramped and hampered. I often have to boil my incantations over a spirit lamp, and even that is becoming difficult--no methylated."

"Not really lucky," said Richard. "In France the smallest pinch of magic seems to make the N.C.O. sick, and that's why I never got my stripe. To keep my hand in, I once did a little stunt with the sergeant's cigarette: it grew suddenly longer as he struck a match to light it, and went on growing till he had to ask me to light it for him, and then it shrank up and burnt his nose. Of course he couldn't really bring the thing home to me, but somehow--well, as I say, I never got my stripe."

To this discussion, and indeed to all the enchantments, Lady Arabel paid no attention, but continued to talk a little nervously on very insipid subjects. Her eyes had the pathetic look often seen in stupid people's eyes, the "Don't-listen-to-me" look, "I am not saying what I should like to say. The real Me is better than this."

Finally Richard indulged in a trick that was evidently a stock joke among magic people, for the witch laughed directly it began. Just as the hostess, with poised fork and spoon, was about to distribute the whitebait, the round table began to spin, and the whitebait were whisked away from her. The table continued to spin for a moment, with a deep thrilling organ sound, and when it stopped, the whitebait were found to have assembled opposite to Richard's place. He distributed them gravely. Lady Arabel turned scarlet, and murmured to Sarah Brown: "So dretfully ingenious, and so merry."

Sarah Brown took pity on her, and began talking at random. The orchestra was busy again, and to the tune of a loud elusive rag-time, she shouted: "Do you know, I gave my job the sack this morning. I shall be on the brink of starvation in three and a half days' time. That's counting a box of Oxo Cubes I have by me. You don't happen to know of a suitable job. I can't cook, and if I sew a button on it comes off quicker than if I hadn't. But I once learnt to play the big drum."

"My dear," said Lady Arabel, instantly motherly. "How too dretful. I wish I knew of something suitable. But--war-time you know,--I'm afraid I shan't be justified in keeping on the orchestra, certainly not in adding to it. Besides, of course, although women are simply too splendid nowadays, don't you think the big drum--just a wee bit unwomanly, my dear. However----"

"Are you clever?" asked Richard.

"Yes, she is," said the witch proudly. "She writes Minor Poetry. I saw a bit by her in a magazine that had no pictures,--the bit of poetry was between an article on Tariff Reform and a statement of the Coal Situation, and it began 'Oh my beloved....' I thought it was a very beautiful bit of Minor Poetry, but somehow I couldn't make it fit in with the two articles. That worried me a little."

"If you'd try your best not to be clever I'd give you a job," said Richard, who with a rather tiresome persistence was now levitating the chicken, so that, invisibly suspended at a height of eighteen inches above the middle of the table, it dripped gravy into a bowl of daffodils. "In fact I will give you a job. I have a farm called Higgins Farm, just about half-way between sea-level and sky-level. You can be a Hand, if you like, at sixpence an hour. You can get there from Mitten Island every day quite easily, and I'll tell you how. It's just the other side of the Parish of Faery, on your right as you reach the mainland from Mitten Island. You follow the Green Ride through the Enchanted Forest, until you come to the Castle where the Young-est Prince--who rescued one of the Fetherstonhaugh girls from a giant and married her--used to live. The Castle's to let now; she is an ambulance driver in Salonika, and he a gunner--just got his battery, I believe. Below the outer wall of the Castle you will see the Daisified Path, and that leads you straight to the gate of Higgins Farm, under a clipped box archway."

"I haven't got a land outfit," said Sarah Brown. "But I saw a pair called Mesopo-tamian Officer's Model, with laces and real white buckskin collision mats between the knees, that would fit me, and I can pawn my----"

At that moment there was a loud report. Every one looked at the double bass, but all his strings were for the moment intact.

"A maroon," said the witch.

"My dears," exclaimed Lady Arabel, much relieved to hear that this new sen-sation was not supernatural. "How too dretfully tahsome with the sweet and the savoury still to come. Do you know, I promised Pinehurst--my husband--never to remain in this house during an air-raid. It was his own fault, the dear thing; he had a craze for windows; this house has more glass space than wall, I think, and Pine-hurst, in his spare time, used always to be making plans for squeezing in more win-dows. Our room is like a conservatory--so dretfully embarrassing. So I always take my knitting across the road to the crypt of St. Sebastian's, and I'm sure you won't mind coming too. You might have brought a box of spellicans, or a set of table cro-quiet, but I'm afraid the Vicar wouldn't like it. A nice man but dretfully particular. We must wait for the end of this piece, the first violin is so touchy."

They all waited patiently while the piece continued. It was a plain uneventful piece, composed by a Higgins relative and therefore admired in the household.

"A thing that puzzles me," said the witch, taking advantage of an emotional pause while one violin was wheezing a very long small note by itself, "is why only ugly songs are really persistent. Haven't you noticed, for instance, that a peacock, or a cat on the wall, or a baby with a tin trumpet, will give their services most generously for hours on end, while a robin on a snowy tree, or a nightingale, or a fairy----"

She was interrupted by a scuffling sound in the umbrella-stand, and Harold the Broomstick, after a moment's rather embarrassing entanglement with a butterfly net, approached, panting.

"I must go," said the witch. "I bet you twopence we shall have some fun to-night. Sarah Brown, I'll come back and fetch you when it's all over."

Lady Arabel and Sarah Brown crossed the road to the church, Richard following a few yards behind.

"I'm afraid my little dinner-party wasn't a great success," said Lady Arabel confidentially. "Rrchud and Angela didn't get that good talk on occult subjects as Meta Ford said they would. Of course Rrchud, as you noticed, was dretfully restless and lighthearted; all boys are like that for the first few hours of their leave. He is naturally of a quiet disposition, though you wouldn't think it from to-night."

There was a distant blot of gunfire on the air, just as they reached the door of the crypt. The very stout dog of the Vicar (are not all reverend dogs fat?) was waiting there with a bored look.

"The Vicar allows no animals inside the crypt. So hard on Mrs. Perry's canary which has fits. I was here once when the Vicar's youngest son brought in a rabbit under his coat. A dretful scene, my dear."

That district of London happened to be rather a courageous one. The inhabitants felt that if the War had to be brought home to them, common politeness dictated that it should find them at home. There were not more than a dozen people in the crypt therefore. Most of them were old ladies from the district's less respectable quarter, knitting. The Vicar was trying to press comfort upon them, but without much success, for they were all quite content, discussing the deaths in their families.

The noise of gunfire was coming nearer, shaking the ground like the uneven tread of a drunken giant. Sarah Brown concentrated on an evening newspaper, busily reading again and again one of those columns of confidential man-to-man advertisement, which everybody reads with avidity while determining the more never to buy the article advertised. But presently the fidgeting hands of Richard caught her eye, and she looked at him. He was sitting next to his mother on a stone step. He seemed to be in a quieter mood and attempted no manifestation. Sarah Brown thought he was suppressing excitement, however, and indeed he presently said: "I say, won't it be fun lying about all this to posterity and Americans, and other defenceless innocents."

Opposite to them, on two campstools, sat a young bridling mother of fifty, with her old hard daughter of sixteen or so. Hard was that daughter in every way; you would have counted her age in winters, not in summers, so obviously untender were her years. An iron plait of hair lay for about six inches down her spine; her feet and ankles made the campstool on which she sat, looking pathetically ethereal. Of such stuff as this is the backbone of England made, which is perhaps why the backbone of England sometimes seems so sadly inflexible.

There was a screeching noise outside, followed by an incredible crash. It seemed to cleave a bottomless abyss between one second and the next, so that one seemed to be conscious for the first time in an astonished and astonishing world.

Lady Arabel said: "Boys will be boys, of course I know, but really this is going a little too far. Pinehurst's one hobby was his windows."

The campstooled mother gave a luxurious little shriek as soon as the crash was safely over. "The villains," she said kittenishly. "Aiming at places of worship as usual. I am absolutely paralysed with terror. Mary, darling, I don't believe you turned a hair."

"Pas un cheval," replied her firm daughter, in not unnatural error. One could easily see that she was beloved at home, and one wondered why.

The sound of the guns seemed only a negative form of sound after the bomb, and clearly above the firing could be heard a howl. The Vicar's dog, still howling, ran into the crypt.

"RUPERT!" said the Vicar, in a terrible voice, interrupting himself in the middle of a cheering platitude. But he had no time to say anything more, for behind Rupert came a procession of perhaps a dozen people, all dressed in sheets. Everybody saw at one pitiful glance that these were unfortunate householders, so suddenly roused from oblivion as to forget all their ordinary suburban dignity, probably barely escaping from ruined homes with their lives and a sheet each. There was a very old man, a middle-aged spinster, and then an enormous group of children of ages varying from two months to twenty years, followed by their parents, teachers, or guardians.

A nearer gun began to fire, and one of the old ladies on the other side of the crypt suddenly threw down her knitting and began confessing her sins. "Ow, I shall go to 'ell," she shouted dramatically. "I bin sich a wicked ol' woman. I nearly done in me first ol' man by biffin' the chopper at 'is nob, and Lawd, the lies I bin an' tol' me second only yesterday."

"This is indeed a solemn moment," said the sheeted spinster sitting down beside Lady Arabel. "I hope I am meeting it in a proper spirit, but of course one is still only human, and naturally nervous. I have learned my statement by heart."

"What statement?" asked Lady Arabel, who was rather deeply engrossed in turning the heel of the sock she was knitting.

"The statement I shall make when the sheep are divided from the goats."

"Oh, come, come," said kind Lady Arabel. "Things are not so bad as that, surely. You must not be so dretfully pessimistic."

"You mistake me," said the sheeted lady, bridling. "There is, I am confident, no cause whatever for pessimism on my part. I have no misgivings as to the verdict. But not being used to courts of law, I thought it best to learn my statement, as I say, by heart."

The old knitter had been rather annoyed to find her confession interrupted. "A wicked ol' woman I may be," she said with more dignity. "But I'll never regret givin' that bloody speshul a bit o' me mind this mornin' when 'e turned saucy to the sugar queue. I ses to 'im----"

"We all have our faults," Lady Arabel's neighbour broke in. "But I think, at this solemn moment, I may feel thankful that hastiness of recrimination was never one of mine. All my life I have made it an unalterable rule never to make a statement without first asking myself: Is it *TRUE*? Is it *JUST*? Is it *KIND*?"

"You may well say so," replied Lady Arabel pleasantly. "I only wish the younger generation would follow your example. Nowadays it is much more likely to be: Is it true? No. Is it just? No. Is it kind? No. Is it *FUNNY*? Yes. And out it comes."

"Be that as it may," said the ladylike creature. (One could see she was a Real Lady even through the sheet. Obviously she read the *Morning Post* daily.) "Be that as it may, perhaps you can help me in one little matter which is intriguing me slightly even at this solemn moment. Do you suppose the sheep will be allowed to hear the trial of the goats, or will the court be cleared? I must say I should be so interested to hear the defence of the late churchwarden who eloped with----"

"Ah, please, please," said Lady Arabel, "don't talk in that dretful way. Don't let your mind dwell on the worst. I assure you that you will be all right."

"Of course I shall be all right, as you put it," said the elderly lady, coldly drawing herself up. "Everybody can be my witness that I have kept my candle burning in my small corner----"

"Good gracious," shrieked the kittenish mother. "A candle burning to-night. And probably unshaded. Don't you know that those fiends in the sky are always on the watch for the slightest illumination?"

"Fiends in the sky!" exclaimed the sheeted lady. "Do you mean to say they are abroad even at this solemn moment?"

"Oh, don't talk such rot," implored the hard flapper. "Who the dickens do you suppose was responsible for that crash?"

"Responsible for the crash!" said the other, whose tones were becoming more and more alive with exclamation marks. "Is then the solemn work of summoning us entrusted to the minions of the Evil One?"

A series of crashes interrupted her, the work of the adjacent gun. The earth shook, and each report was followed by the curious ethereal wail of shells on their way.

"What, again?" exclaimed Lady Arabel's sheeted neighbour. "I should have thought one would have been ample. But still, one cannot be too careful, and some people are heavy sleepers. I heard the first myself without any possibility of mistake, and rose at once, though the slab lay heavy on my chest----"

"Most unwise," said Lady Arabel, "to touch that sort of thing late at night. I always have a little Benger myself."

Sarah Brown happened to look at Richard. His eyes were shut, but he was smiling very broadly with tight lips, and his face was turned towards the ceiling. His fingers were very tense and busy on his lap, as though he were still fidgeting with magic. But her study of him was interrupted by the loud denouncing voice of the very venerable man who had led the procession of late-comers.

"A dog in this hallowed place," he said, pointing at the deeply disconcerted Rupert who was weaving himself nervously in and out of his master's legs. "Never in all the forty years of my ministration here have I allowed such an outrage----"

"Gently, gently, my dear sir," protested the Vicar, a little roused. "I am the minister of this church, and the dog is mine. I was indeed about to turn it out when you entered, after which I lost sight of it for a moment. Rupert, go home."

Rupert howled again, and lay down as if about to faint.

"Forty years have I been Vicar of this parish," said the veteran, "and never----"

"What?" interrupted the Vicar, "Forty years Vicar of this parish. Then you must be Canon Burstley-Ripp. How very extraordinary, I always understood that he passed away quite ten years ago."

He approached the old man and strove to button-hole him. The sheet at first foiled him in this intention, but he presently contented himself with seizing a little corner of it, by which he led his aged brother vicar into a corner. There they could be heard for some time misunderstanding each other in low earnest tones.

"Ow, what a wicked ol' woman I bin an' bin," suddenly burst forth again the repentant knitter. "I bin an' stole 'arf a pound o' sugar off of the Eelite 'Atshop where I does a bit o' cleanin'. Ef I get out o' this alive, I swear I'll repay it an 'undredfold--that is ef I can get that much awf me sugar card...."

Sarah Brown was becoming sleepy. A blankness was invading her mind, and the talk in the crypt seemed to lose its meaning, and to consist chiefly of S's. She pondered idly on the family of children with their elders, all of whom were now studying each other with a certain look of disillusionment. It was a group whose relationships were difficult to make out, the ages of many of the children being unnaturally approximate. There seemed to be at least seven children under three years old, and yet they all bore a strong and regrettable family likeness. Several of the babies would hardly have been given credit for having reached walking age, yet none had been carried in. The woman who seemed to imagine herself the mother of this rabble was distributing what looked like hurried final words of advice. The father with a pensive eye was obviously trying to remember their names, and at intervals whispering to a man apparently twenty years his senior, whom he addressed as Sonny. It was all very confusing.

A long dim stretch of time seemed to have passed when suddenly the note of a bugle sprang out across space. Somehow the air at once felt cooler and more wholesome, the sound of the All-clear had something akin to the sight of the sun after a thunderstorm, lighting up a crouching whipped world.

"The Trump at last," said Lady Arabel's garrulous neighbour, rising with alacrity, and twitching her sheet into more becoming folds. "I was just wondering----"

But at that moment the two Vicars approached, and the elder one, including both the spinster and the mysterious family in one glance, spoke in a clerical yet embarrassed voice.

"Dear friends, a slight but inconvenient mistake has occurred, and I am afraid I must ask you to submit blindly to my guidance in a matter strangely difficult to explain, even as I--myself in much confusion--bow to the advice of my reverend friend here. It would be out of place----"

The spinster interrupted, and, by the way she did it, one saw that she was Chapel. "Excuse me, Canon," she said acidly, "but is not all discussion out of place at this solemn moment?"

"Believe me, madam," replied the aged Burstley-Ripp. "You overrate the solemnity of the moment. I must earnestly ask you all to return with me to the places whence--labouring under an extraordinary error--we came to-night. I see that Mrs. Parachute trusts me, and is prepared to lead her little flock to rest again. You, madam----"

"Where Mrs. Parachute leads, far be it from me to seem behindhand," said the other, much ruffled, as she gathered her sheet about her. By the way she said it, one saw that she and Mrs. Parachute did not call. She bowed to Lady Arabel, and became satirical, even arch. "Good afternoon, Mrs.--er--, I am assured that the moment is not solemn, and therefore solemn it shall not be. To turn to lighter subjects, I hope I shall have the pleasure of meeting you and your delightful son and daughter again at no distant date, the moment then being genuinely solemn. I fear I have no visiting card on me, but--er--perhaps my slab just outside--very superior granite--would do as a substitute...."

The pale party filed out of the crypt and disappeared. The remaining Vicar smote his brow, and addressed the now calm Rupert in a low voice, but with such unaccountable warmth that that harassed animal disappeared precipitately in the direction of his home.

Lady Arabel, Sarah Brown, and Richard crossed the churchyard together.

"Oh, my dears, look," said Lady Arabel. "How too too dretful, that bomb fell quite close to us. Do look how it has disturbed the graves...."

CHAPTER VI
AN AIR RAID SEEN FROM ABOVE

The moonlight lay like cream upon the pavement when the witch and Harold her broomstick left the Higgins' doorstep. London was a still Switzerland in silver and star-grey, unblotted by people. There was a hint of pale green about the moonlight, and the lamps with their dim light downcast were like daffodils in faery fields.

The witch mounted. Harold, who was every inch a thoroughbred and very highly strung, trembled beneath her, but not with fear. They reached Piccadilly Circus with supernatural speed, and flashed across it. The sound of people singing desultorily while taking shelter in the Tube floated up to them. Here the witch said "Yoop" to Harold, and he reared and shot upwards, narrowly missing the statue of One In A Bus-catching Attitude, which marks the middle of the Circus.

As soon as the witch had out-distanced the noise of expectant London, she heard quite distinctly the approach of London's guests. They came with a chorus of many notes, all deep and dangerous.

There were a few clouds wandering about among the stars, and to one of these the witch and her faithful Harold repaired. A cloud gives quite reasonable support to magic people, and most witches and wizards have discovered the delight of paddling knee-deep about those quicksilver continents. They wander along shining and changing valleys under a most ardent sky; they climb the purple thunderclouds, or launch the first snowflake of a blizzard; they spring from pink stepping-stone to pink stepping-stone of clouds each no bigger than a baby's hand, across great sunsets. Often when in London I am battling with a barrage of rain, or falling over unseen strangers into gutters during fogs, I think happily of the sunlit roof of cloud above my head, and of the witches and wizards, lying on their backs with their coats off, among cloud-meadows in a glory of perfect summer and sun.

The witch, with one soothing hand on the bristling mane of her Harold, lay on her front on the cloud she had chosen, and looked down through a little hole in it. It was practically the only cloud present that would have afforded reasonable cover; the others were mere wisps of sky-weed floating in the moonlight.

There was a greater chorus of aeroplanes below her now; the whole sky was ringing with it. The witch could hear a deep bass-voiced machine, a baritone, a quavering tenor, and--thin and sharp as a pin--a little treble sound that made Harold rear and struggle to be free.

"Another witch," said the witch. "I was wondering why the Huns hadn't got their magic organised by now." She mounted her Harold and slipped off the cloud.

The guns were shouting now, and the shells wailed and burst not so very far below them, but Harold trembled no longer. More quickly than a falling star he swooped, and in a second the alien witch was in sight, an unwieldy figure whose broomstick sounded rather broken-winded, probably owing to the long-distance flight and to the fourteen stone of Teutonic magic on its back. There was a wicked-looking apparatus attached to the collar of the German broomstick, obviously designed to squirt unpleasant enchantments downward. This contrivance was apparently giving some trouble, for the German was so busy attending to it that at first she did not see or hear the approach of Harold and his rider. She was aroused to her danger by a heavy chunk of magic which struck and nearly unseated her. In a second, however, she was ready with a parrying enchantment, and the fight began. The two broomsticks reared and circled round each other, and over and under each other. From their riders' finger-tips magic of the most explosive kind crackled, and incantations of such potency were exchanged that, I am told, the tiles and chimney-pots of the streets below suffered a good deal. Round and round and over and under whirled the broomsticks, till the very spaces went mad, and London seemed to rush down nightmare slopes into a stormy sky, while its lights swung from pole to pole and were entangled with the stars.

Both broomsticks were by now so uproariously excited that neither witch was able to aim her magic missiles very carefully, and indeed it was not long before Harold passed entirely beyond control. After bucking violently once or twice, he gave a wild high cry that was like the wind howling through the fierce forest past of his race, and fell upon the other broomstick, fixing his bristles into its throat. The shock of the collision was too much for both witches. Our witch--if I may call her so--was shot over Harold's head, and landed on the ample breast of her adversary, who, in consequence, lost her balance. They fell together into space.

"Oh, lost, lost, ..." cried our witch, and thoughts rushed through her mind of green safe places, and old safe years, and the little hut in a pale bluebell wood, where she was born. She had time to remember the blue ground, dimpled and starred with sunlight, and the way the bees pulled over the bluebells and swung on them to the tune of cuckoos in a May mist; she had time to think of the green globe ghosts of the bluebells that haunted the wood after the spring was dead. Bluebells and being young were in all her thoughts, and it was some time before she noticed how slowly she and her enemy were falling.

For they were locked together. And the enemy witch's cloak, an orthodox witch cloak except for its colour, which was German field-grey instead of red, was spread out like a parachute, and was supporting them upon their peaceful and almost affectionate descent.

For all I know they might have alighted gently in the Strand, and the authorities might by now be regretting the capture of a most embarrassing and unaccountable prisoner. But something intervened. The cloud, like a sheep suffering from the lack of other sheep to follow, had not yet quitted the scene. The witches' battle had tended upward, and it had ended several hundred feet above the level of the cloud, which was apparently sinking. The downward course of the combatants' fall was therefore arrested, and they found themselves still interlocked, prostrate and embedded, with their eyes and mouths full of woolly wisps of cloud.

Our witch was the first to recover herself. She stood up and brushed herself, remarking: "By jove, that parachute cloak of yours is a great dodge. I wish I'd thought of it. I always keep my full-dress togs put away, like the ass that I am. A stitch or two, and a few lengths of whalebone would have done the trick."

The German was an older woman, and less adaptable to the strange chances of War. She was silent for a few minutes, seated in the small crater made in the cloud by her fall. She was not exactly ugly. She had the sort of face about which one could not help feeling that one could have done it better oneself, or at least that one could have taken more trouble. It seemed moulded--even kneaded--carelessly, in very soft material. Beneath her open cloak her dress was of the ordinary German *Reform-Kleid* type, and her figure had the rather jelloid appearance of those who affect this style. Her regulation witch's hat was by now, probably, in the Serpentine, and her round head was therefore disclosed, with two stout sand-coloured plaits pursuing each other round it.

The witches faced each other for some seconds. A long way away they could hear the spitting and crackling sound of the two broomsticks fighting. Looking up, they could see the combatants, like black comets in collision. Our witch, who had good sight, saw that the enemy broomstick was upper-most, and that the writhing Harold was being shaken like a mouse. Their bristles were interlocked. One twig floated down between the witches, and our witch recognised it as coming from her poor Harold's mane. As, for this purpose, she brought her eyes to her immediate surroundings, it seemed to her suddenly that the sky was growing larger, and then she realised that this was because their refuge was growing smaller. The edges of the cloud were dissolving. She saw at last her peril and her disadvantage. If Harold should be killed or disabled she could never reach the earth again, except by means of a fatal fall of several thousand feet. The enemy witch, with her ingenious cloak contrivance strapped securely about her, stood a reasonable chance of escape. But our witch was an amateur in War, she was without support, forlornly dressed in her faithful blue serge three-year-old, and her little squirrel tippet.

Magic, as you know, has limitations. Fire is of course a plaything in magic hands. Water has its docile moments, the earth herself may be tampered with, and an incantation may call man or any of his possessions to attention. But space is too great a thing, space is the inconceivable Hand, holding aloft this fragile delusion that is our world. There is no power that can mock at space, there is no enchantment that is not lost between us and the moon, and all magic people know--and tremble to know--that in a breath, between one second and another, that Hand may close, and the shell of time first crack and then be crushed, and magic be one with nothingness and death and all other delusions. This is why magic, which treats the other elements as its servants, bows before space, and has to call such a purely independent contrivance as a broomstick to its help in the matter of air-travel.

The witches faced each other on their little unstable sanctuary in the kingdom of space. Our witch felt secretly sick, and at the same time she tore fear from her mind, and knew that death was but an imperfectly kept secret, and that not an evil one. After all, we have condemned it unheard.

Both witches could talk a magic tongue, and make themselves mutually understood. Neither knew the other's natural tongue. But when our witch noticed several large ferocious tears rolling down her opponent's cheeks, she was able, by means of magic, to say: "Great Scott, my good person, what are you crying for?"

"I am not crying," replied the German witch. "I would not allow one tear of mine to fall upon and water one possible grain of wheat in this accursed country of yours. Certainly I am not crying."

"Accursed country?" echoed the astounded English witch. "How d'you mean--accursed? This is England, you know. England hasn't done anything accursed. Aren't you muddling it up with Germany?"

"England is the World Enemy," said the German, evidently pleased to meet someone to whom this information was fresh. "Throughout the ages she has been the Robber State, crushing the weaker nations, adding to her own wealth by treachery, and now forcing this war of aggression upon her peace-loving neighbours."

Our witch laughed. She was forgetting her danger. "This is really rather funny," she said. "Do you know what's happened? You've been reading the **Daily Mail** and misunderstanding it. The whole of that quotation applied to Germany, not England. It's Germany that's being naughty. You made a mistake, but never mind, I won't repeat it."

The German took no notice of this. The past three years had made her an adept in taking no notice.

"And now," she added. "After all these weary months of hoping, and long-distance broomstick practice, and of parachute practice, and of conflict with narrow officialdom, I have come--and this is the result. I am separated from my broomstick, which has all the germ-bombs hanging from its collar--the germs are those of dissension and riot--I am marooned upon an English cloud, with no enemy at my mercy but a paltry and treacherous non-combatant----"

"At your mercy," breathed our witch, remembering. She looked up. The broomsticks were closer now, and through the breathless air, amidst the dream-like firing of the guns below, she could hear the difficult gasping of the hard-pressed Harold, still fighting bravely but with hardly a twig on his head.

The tide of space was coming in. The edge of the cloud was barely six inches from her hand. Our witch's mind overflowed with the thought of invasions and the coming in of tides. It seemed that all her life she had been living on a narrowing shore. She remembered all her dawns as precarious footholds of peace on a threatened rock, and all her evenings as golden sands sloping down into encroaching sleep. She realised Everything as a little hopeless garrison against the army of Nothing.

She clutched a pinch of cloud nervously, and it broke off in her hand. She recalled her senses with a devastating effort.

"Do you mean to say," she said, after a moment, "that poor dear Germany really believes that she is right and we are wrong? I suppose, when you come to think of it, a man-eating tiger feels the same way. It fights with a high heart, and a hot reproach, just as we do----"

"We are Crusaders," said the German. "Crusaders at War with Evil."

"Why, how funny--so are we," said our witch. "But then how very peculiar that two Crusaders should apparently be fighting each other. Where then is the Evil? In No Man's Land?"

"We are fighting," recited the German glibly, "because England is the World Enemy. Throughout the ages she has been the Rob----"

There was a violent explosion quite close to them, and the cloud reeled and shook. About a foot of the German end of it broke off and was dissolved.

"We're within range of our guns," said our witch, looking down. "This cloud must be sinking."

"It will never sink enough to save you," said the German, trying to conceal the nervousness with which she rearranged her rigid-looking cloak round her. She seemed to be sinking herself to a certain extent; perhaps the warmth of her emotions was melting the cloud beneath her. Certainly she now sat, apparently squat as an idol, her figure submerged in cloud to the waist.

The English witch looked down, singing a little to keep up her *morale*. London looked exactly like the maps you buy for sixpence from sad-looking gentlemen in the Strand, only it was sown with a thin crop of lights, and was chiefly designed in grey and darker grey, and the Tubes did not show so indecently. With surprising clearness the rhythmic whispering of the trains and the scanty traffic could be heard, and once even the shrill characteristic voice of an ambulance. Somehow space did not seem disturbed by these sounds; its quietness pressed upon the listeners' minds like a heavy dream, and there was no real believing in anything but space. Our witch felt she could have smudged London off the face of space with her finger, and the thought of seven million lives involved in the fate of that sliding chart carried no conviction to her. She forced into her mind the realisation of humanity, and of little lives lived in little rooms.

"As one Crusader to another," she said, "do you find it does much good in the war against Evil to drop bombs on people in their homes? After all, every baby is good in bed, and even soldiers when on leave are anti-militarist."

"It always does good to exterminate vermin in their lair," said the German, trying restlessly to raise herself more to the level of her lighter companion, who was still perched on the surface of the cloud. "It is at home that Evil is originated, it is at home that English women conceive and bear a new generation of enemies of the Right, it is at home that English children are bred up in their marauding ways. It is on the home, the vital place of Evil, that the scourge should fall."

"Oh, but surely not," said our witch eagerly. "It is at home that people are kindly and think what they will have for supper, and bathe their babies. Men come home when they are hurt or hungry, and women when they are lonely or tired. Nobody is taught anything stupid or international at home. You can bring death to a home, but never a righteous scourge. Nobody feels scourged or instructed by a bomb in their parlour, they just feel dead, and dead without a reason."

The cloud was very small now. The filmy edges of it were faintly rising and falling like the seaweed frill of a rock in the sea. The witch kept her eyes on her opponent's face, because to look anywhere else gave her a white feeling in her head.

"Crusades of the high explosive kind," she said, "can work only on battle-fields. Indeed, even on battle-fields--ah, what are we about, what are we about? We are neither of us killing Evil, we are killing youth...."

"I know, I know," wept the German witch. "My wizard fell at Vimy Ridge...."

"You are talking magic at last," said our witch. "Dear witch, why don't you go home and ask how it can be a good plan for one Crusader against Evil to blow up another? How can two people be righteously scourging each other at the same time? It is like the old problem of two serpents eating each other, starting at the tail. There must be some misunderstanding somewhere. Or else some real Evil somewhere."

"There is," said the German, recovering herself. "England is Evil. England is the World Enemy. Throughout the ages she has been the Robber State, crushing----"

But she had little luck. Once more she was interrupted by an explosion, a much louder one, directly above them. Our witch hardly heard the noise; she seemed suddenly to have found the climax of her life, and the climax was pain. There was pain and a feeling of terrible change all over her, smothering her, and a super-pain in her shoulder. After a second or two as long as death, she realised dimly that she was all tensely strung to an attitude, like a marionette. Her hands were up trying to shield her head, her chin was pressed down to her drawn-up knees. Her blue serge shoulder was extraordinarily wet and immovable. She looked along the cloud. Her enemy was not there. There was a round hole in the cloud, and as she leaned painfully towards it, she could see a few of the lights of London, and something falling spasmodically towards them.

The cloud had been shaken to its foundations by the two explosions, and the German witch, who had been seated perhaps on a seam in the material, or at any rate on one of the less stable parts of the fabric, had fallen through. Her parachute cloak, in passing through the hole in the cloud, had been turned inside out above her head, and rendered useless. Over and about her falling figure her broomstick darted helplessly, uttering curious sad cries, like a seagull's.

Even as the English witch watched her enemy's disaster, the larger part of the cloud, weakened by all the shock and movement, broke away with a hissing sound. The witch's feet hung now over space, she dared not move; she had difficulty in steadying herself with her unwounded arm, for her hand could find only a quicksand of dissolving cloud to lean on. She had no thoughts left but thoughts of danger and of pain.

But Harold the Broomstick came back. The witch heard a rustling sound close to her, and it startled her more than all the noise of the guns, which had come, as it seemed, from the forgotten other side of eternity. The rough head of Harold appeared over the cloud's edge, and insinuated itself pathetically under her arm. Very carefully and very painfully the witch reached a kneeling position, damaging her refuge with every movement in spite of her care. She gasped with pain, and Harold tried to look very strong and hopeful to comfort her. He straightened his back, and she crawled into the saddle. The tremor of their launching split the cloud into several parts, which disintegrated. There was no more foot-hold on it; the tide had come up and submerged it.

Harold the Broomstick was crippled, he stumbled as he flew, sometimes he dropped a score of feet, and span. He did stunts by mistake.

They had not strength enough between them to get home. They made a forced landing in the silver loneliness of Kensington Gardens. It was a fortunate place, for there is much magic there. Wherever there are children who pretend, there grows a little magic in the air, and therefore the wind of Kensington Gardens thrills with enchantment, and the Round Pond, full of much pretence of great Armadas, crossed and re-crossed with the abiding wakes of ships full of treasure and romance, is a blessed lake to magic people.

The witch bathed Harold, her broomstick, in the Round Pond. He evidently felt its healing quality at once, for after the first minute of immersion, he swam about exultantly, and shook drops full of moonlight out of his mane.

The bugles sounded All-clear in many keys all round the ear's horizon; their sound matched the waning moonlight.

The witch bathed her shoulder, and then she found her way to a little quiet place she knew of, where no park-keeper ever looks, a place where secret and un-gardened daffodils grow in springtime, a place where all the mice and birds play unafraid, because no cat can find the way thither. You can see the Serpentine from that place, and the bronze shadows under its bridge, but no houses, and no railways, and no signs of London.

Here the witch made a little fire, and leaned three sticks together over it; she lighted the fire with her finger-tip and hung over it the little patent folding caul-dron, which she always carried on a chatelaine swinging from her belt. And she made a charm of daisy-heads, and spring-smelling grasses, and the roots of unap-preciated weeds, and the mosses that cover the tiny faery cliffs of the Serpentine. Over the mixture she shook out the contents of one of her little paper packets of magic. All this she boiled over her fire for many hours, sitting beside it in the silver darkness, with her knees drawn up and her hands clasped in front of them. The trees sprang up into the moonlight like dark fountains from the pools of their own shadows. Little shreds of cloud flowed wonderfully across the sky. There was no sound except the sound of the water, like an uncertain player upon a little instrument. The charm was still unfinished when the dawn passed over London, and the sun came up, the seed of another day, sown in a rich red soil. The trees of the Gardens remembered their daylight shadows again, and forgot their mystery. The water-birds, after examining their shoulder-blades with minute care for some moments, launched themselves upon a lake of diamonds. There seemed a veil of mist and bird-song over the world. The sudden song of the birds was like finding the hearing of one's heart restored, after long deafness.

The witch anointed her shoulder with the charm, after having first made a drop of potion out of the bubbles in it. This potion she drank, and was healed of her wound and her weariness, and of all desires except a desire to sleep with her face among the daffodils. She was the most beautifully alone person in the world that morning; nobody could have found her. A thin string of very blue smoke went up from her faint fire and was tangled among the boughs of a flowering tree, but the coarse eye of a park-keeper could never have seen it. She had escaped from the net of the cruel hours; for her the stained world was washed clean; for her all horror held its breath; for her there was absolute spring, and an innocent sun, and the shadows of daffodils upon closed eyes....

CHAPTER VII
THE FAERY FARM

Sarah Brown, finding herself unfetched by the witch, went home alone as soon as the 'buses began putting out to sea after the storm. She expected to find the witch at home, but only the Dog David and Peony were in the House of Living Alone. David lay on Peony's bed, and Peony under it. Sarah Brown saw them as she passed their open door.

"Ow Marmaduke!" said Peony, "is it all over? Are you sure? Them 'uns is so bloody deceitful you never know but what they might go an' blow a bugle or two to mike believe they'd done, an' then drops bombs on us just as we was comin' 'appily out from under our beds."

Peony, with a touching faith in the combined protective powers of twelve inches of mattress and nine inches of dog, had been reading a little paper book called **Love in Society** by the light of an electric torch.

"It's all truly over," said Sarah Brown, who had come home through a roar of rumour. "They say we've brought down at least one Boche. In fact the ferryman says his aunt telephoned that the special on her corner says a female Boche was brought down. But that hardly sounds likely. Hasn't the witch come home yet?"

"Lawd no," replied Peony. "The dear ol' Soup never comes 'ome of a moonlight night. It's my belief she goes to Maiden'ead among the Jews, to keep out of the wiy, and 'oo's to blime 'er?"

"Well, that's all right," said Sarah Brown. "For now I shall be able to buy-- without pawning anything for the moment--a little land outfit from stock. I know she has some."

The night was by then far from young, in fact it was well into its second childhood. But Sarah Brown and the Dog David sought and tried on land outfits for several hours.

The shop was divided into three horizontal departments. Nearest the floor were the foodstuffs; biscuit tins buttressed the counter on every side; regiments of Grape-nuts, officered by an occasional Quaker Oat, stood in review order all round the lower shelves. On the counter little castles of tinned fruit were built, while bins beneath it held the varied grain, cereal, and magic stock. About on a level with one's head the hardware department began: frying-pans lolled with tin coffee-pots over racks, dust-pans divorced from their brushes were platonically attached to flat-irons or pie-dishes, Stephen's Inks were allied with penny mugs or tins of boot polish in an invasion of the middle shelves, and a wreath of sponges crowned the champion of a row of kettles in shining armour. Against the ceiling the drapery section was found. Overalls, ready-made breeches, babies' socks, and pink flannel-ette mysteries hung doubled up as if in pain over strings nailed to the rafters. From this department Sarah Brown, balanced upon three large biscuit tins placed on the counter, chose her outfit with vanity and care. The general effect was not good, but she did not know this, for she studied the parts separately in a six-inch mirror. She was filled with a simple pleasure. For she was always absurdly moved by little excitements, and by any prospect of a changed to-morrow. She was not really used to being alive at all, and that is what made her take to magic so kindly.

"In six hours," she said, "I shall be on my way to something utterly new."

And in six hours she was on her way, whistling, across the Parish of Faery. The Dog David ran in front of her among the daisies. The rabbits can never be caught in this land of happy animals, but they give good sport and always play fair.

David Blessing Brown, a dog of independent yet loving habit, had spent about four-fifths of his life in the Brown family. He was three years old, and though in-eligible for military service, made a point of wearing khaki about his face, and in a symmetrical heart shaped spot near his tail. To Sarah Brown he was the Question and the Answer, his presence was a constant playtime for her mind; so well was he loved that he seemed to her to move in a little mist and clamour of love. With ev-ery one else she held but lame intercourse, but her Dog David and she withheld no passing thought from each other. They could often be heard by unmattering land-ladies and passers-by exchanging views in the strong Suffolk accent that was a sort of standing joke between them. I believe that Sarah Brown had loved the Dog David so much that she had given him a soul. Certainly other dogs did not care for him. David said that they had found out that his second name was Blessing, and that they laughed at him for it. His face was seamed with the scars of their laughing. But I know that the enmity had a more fundamental reason than that. I know that when men speak with the tongues of angels they are shunned and hated by men, and so I think that when dogs approach humanity too nearly they are banished from the love of their own kind.

Sarah Brown was not altogether unfamiliar with the Parish of Faery, but she never failed to be surprised by the enchantment of the Enchanted Forest. The Green Ride runs straight through it, so incredibly straight that as you walk along it the end of it is at the end of your sight, and is like a star in a green sky. There is a dream that binds your mind as you cross the forest; it is like an imitation of eternity, so that, as you pass into the forest's shade, time passes from before you, and, as you pass out of it, you seem to have lived a thousand quiet and utterly forgotten lives. Clocks and calendars have no meaning in the forest; the seasons and the hours haunt it at their will, and abide by no law. Just as the sun upon a stormy day makes golden a moving and elusive acre in our human woods, so the night in the Enchanted Forest comes and goes like a ghost upon the sight of lovers of the night. For there you may step, unastonished, from the end of a day into its beginning; there the summer and the winter may dodge each other round one tree; there you may see at one glance a spring hoar frost and an autumn trembling of airs, a wild cherry tree blossoming beside a tawny maple. The forest is so deep and so thick that it provides its own sky, and can enjoy its own impulses, and its own quiet anarchy. There you forget that sky of ours across whose face some tyrant drives our few docile seasons in conventional order.

I think the Dog David in his own way shared the dream that leads wayfarers through the Enchanted Forest. When he came out with Sarah Brown under the tasselled arch of Travellers' Joy that crosses the end of the Green Ride, he was all shining and dewy with adventure, and his tail was upright, as though he were pretending that it carried a flag.

On an abrupt hill in the middle of an enormous green meadow a Castle stood, just as Richard had predicted. It was To Let, and was not looking its best. Some man of enterprise, taking advantage of its forlorn condition, had glued an advertisement upon its donjon keep. You could almost have measured that advertisement in acres; it recommended a face cream, and represented a lady with a face of horrible size, whose naturally immaculate complexion was marred by the rivets and loopholes of the donjon keep itself, which protruded in rather a distressing way.

Oak trees stood round the foot of that pale hill, and the general effect was rather that of parsley round a ham.

Between two oaks Sarah Brown, following directions, found the beginning of the Daisified Path. There were not only daisies all over the path but real violets on either side of it. The daisies looked one in the face, but the violets did not, because they had morbidly bad manners. Still of course manners are very small change and count for very little; the violet, being an artist, is entitled to any manners it likes, while the daisy has no temperament whatever, and no excuse for eccentricity. Grasshoppers tatted industriously and impartially among the daisies and the violets.

Here outside the forest there was weather again, and the weather was more promising than generous. It continued to promise all day without exactly explaining what its promise was, and without achieving any special fulfilment. Fine silver lines of sunlight were ruled at a steep angle across a grey slate view.

At the gate of Higgins Farm, Sarah Brown was a little disconcerted to find a small dragon. It was coiled round a tree beside the clipped box archway. It was not a very fine specimen, being of a brownish-green colour, and having lost the tip of one wing. Its spine was serrated, especially deeply between its shoulder blades, where it could raise a sort of crest if angered or excited. But at present it was asleep, its saturnine and rather wistful face rested upon one scaly paw.

Sarah Brown was uncertain what to do, but the Dog David took the matter into his own paws by mistake. He had just met one of the castle dogs, one of those tremulous-tailed creatures who spend themselves in a rather pathetic effort to sustain an imaginary reputation for humour. David retorted to this dog's first facetious onslaught with a kindly quip, they trod on each other once or twice with extravagant gestures, and then parted hysterically, each supposing himself to be pursued by the other. It was then that David tripped over the dragon's barbed tail. David squeaked, and the dragon awoke. It uncoiled itself suddenly like a broken spring.

"Gosh," it said. "Asleep again! I was waiting for you, and the sun on my back always makes me sleepy. I am the foreman. Higgins telephoned that you were coming."

It preceded her through the little green archway that led to the farm. The sight reminded Sarah Brown of watching from Golders Green Tube Station the train one has just missed dive into the tunnel. She followed.

On the other side of the archway the whole view of the plain called Higgins Farm met the adventurer. The farm-buildings were heaped graciously together on a little wave in the sea of ploughed fields. Except for two pale ricks in their midst, they exactly matched their surroundings, they were plastered dark red, and thatched with very old green and brown thatch. Beyond the buildings was a little wood, its interior lighted up with bluebells, and this wood merged into an orchard, where a white pony and an auburn pig strove apparently to eat the same blade of grass. The various sections of the farm land lay mapped out in different intensities of brown, very young green, and maturer green, and each section was dotted with people. They seemed small people even from a distance, and, as Sarah Brown advanced at the tail of the dragon, she saw that the workers were all indeed under ordinary human size. The tallest, a man guiding a miniature plough behind a tall horse, might have reached Sarah Brown's shoulder. None of them seemed hard at work, they stood talking in little groups. One group as they passed it was trafficking in cigarette cards. "I want to get my Gold Scale set of English Kings complete," a voice was saying tragically. "Has nobody got Edward the Confessor?" None of them took any notice of the foreman.

"I'm afraid I haven't got the gift of discipline," sighed the dragon. "And fairies are of course abnormally undisciplined creatures. Still, we simply can't get any one else, and Higgins will not apply for a few German prisoners. Get on with your work, you people, do. There, you see, they defy me to an extent. Ever since the cowmen dipped me in the horse-pond my authority's gone--gone where the good niggers go."

I find that there are quite a lot of people who cannot say the word "gone" without adding the clause about the good niggers. These people have vague minds, sown like an allotment with phrases in grooves. Directly the dragon said "to an extent" without qualifying the extent, one saw why it had no gift of discipline.

"I wouldn't attempt this job," it continued, winding breathlessly along the rutty road, "only I am under a great obligation to Richard Higgins. I am a ***protidgy*** of his, you know, he rescued me from a lot of mischievous knights who were persecuting me. One of them had tied his tin hat to my tail, I remember, and the rest were trying to stick their nasty spears between my scales. Really, you know, it was quite dangerous. I have known a fellow's eye put out that way. I am not very good at fighting, though I might have tackled one at a time. Richard Higgins rode right into the midst of them, knocking them right and left. Gosh, he gave them a talking to, and they slank away. He took my case up after that, made enquiries, and gave me this job. We scrape along somehow, but I'm afraid I'm not really suited for it."

They reached a part of a field in which broad beans were enjoying an innocent childhood among white butterflies.

"If you wouldn't mind," said the dragon shyly, "I should like you to hoe between the rows of these beans. You will find a hoe against the big stack. This is your row, I reserved it for you."

All the other rows were occupied by fairy women with their skirts tucked up-- for only your amateur land-woman wears breeches. They all had hoes, but were not using them much. They were singing curious old round songs like summer dreams; you could hear strange fragments of phrases passing from voice to voice. They took no notice of Sarah Brown, and she began to work.

"Oh, my One," she said to David. "How happy this is. No wonder they sing. Any one must sing working like this in great fields. Why, I even remember that the Shropshire Lad whistled once by mistake, while ploughing, on his own admission, until a fatalistic blackbird recalled him to his usual tragic mind."

David sat uncomfortably on a broad bean, protesting against this new mania. For a moment he had thought that she was seeking for a mouse with some patent mouse-finding implement. He had even tried to help her, and turned over a clod with a critical paw, but one sniff had showed him the empty futility of the thing.

Sarah Brown hoed rather happily for a couple of hours, and then she began to count the beans still waiting trustfully in the queue, waiting to be attended to and freed from their embarrassments. There were ninety-six, she decided, standing up ostensibly to greet an aeroplane. She became very glad of the occasional aeroplanes that crossed above her field, and gave her an excuse for standing with a straight back to watch them. Aeroplanes, crossing singly or in wild-bird formations, are so common in the sky of Faery that every one in those parts, while turning his own eyes inevitably upwards, secretly thinks his neighbour lamentably rustic and unsophisticated for looking at them.

Every aeroplane that crosses Faery feels, I suppose, the reflected magic from the land below, for there is never one with the barest minute to spare that does not pause and try to be clever over Higgins Farm. You may see one industriously climbing the clouds over the Enchanted Forest, evidently trying hard to be intent on its destination. You may see it falter, struggling with its sense of duty, and then break weakly into a mild figure eight. The ragged rooks of Faery at once hurry into the air to show their laborious imitator how this should be done. The spirit of frivolous competition enters into the aeroplane, its duty is flung to the winds. It flaunts itself up and down once or twice, as if to say: "Now look, everybody, I'm going to be clever." Then it goes mad. It leaps upon imaginary Boches, it stands upon its head and falls downward until the very butterflies begin to take cover, it stands upon its tail and falls upward, it writes messages in a flowing hand across the sky and returns to cross the t's. It circles impertinently round your head, fixing its bold tricolour eye upon you until you begin to think there must be something wrong with your appearance. It bounds upon a field of onions and rebounds in the same breath from the topmost cloud of heaven. The rooks return disconsolately to their nests.

Then you may see the erring machine suddenly remember itself, and check itself in the act of some new paroxysm. It remembers the European War that gave it birth; it thinks of its mates scanning the sky for its coming; its frivolity ebbs suddenly. The eastern sky becomes once more its highway instead of its trapeze. It collects its wits, emits a few contrite bubbles of smoke, and leaps beyond sight.

Whenever this happened, the female fairies behaved in a very plebeian and forward manner, waving their hoes at each machine, encouraging it by brazen gestures to further extravagances, and striving to reach its hearing with loud shrill cries. There was very little difference between these fairies and other lady war-workers. In fact they were only distinguishable by their stature and by the empty and innocent expression of their faces. Also perhaps by their tuneful singing, and by a habit of breaking out suddenly into country dances between the bean-rows.

Sarah Brown, who worked a great deal more industriously than any one else in sight, soon overtook them, and while conscious of that touch of interested scorn always felt by the One towards the Herd, found relief in watching their vagaries, and presently in speaking to them.

For she needed relief, poor Sarah Brown, her disabilities were catching her up; a hoarse contralto cough was reminding her of many doctors' warnings against manual work. She could feel, so to speak, the distant approaching tramp of that pain in her side under whose threat she had lived all her life. But there were seventy-five beans yet.

The note of her hoe, a high note not quite true pitched, clamoured monotonously upon her brain. Three blisters and a half were persecuting her hands.

"Let them blist," she said defiantly. "This row of beans was given me to hoe, and Death itself shall not take it from me."

She could almost imagine she saw Death, waiting for her tactfully beyond the last bean. She had no sense of proportion. She was so very weary of having her life interrupted by her weakness that anything that she had begun to do always seemed to her worth finishing, even under torture. To finish every task, in spite of all hindrance, was her only ambition, but it was almost always frustrated.

Seventy more beans. "Three score and ten," thought Sarah Brown. "What's that? Only a lifetime." She bent to her work.

A great clump of buttercups bestrode her bean row, and as after a struggle she dragged its protesting roots from the earth, something fell from it.

"Oh, a nest," she gasped. "Look, I have hoed up a nest."

"Good gracious," exclaimed a fairy. "Look what she's done. It's Clement's nest, poor chap, he only married in February. Say, girls, here's Clement's semi-detached gone up."

Cries of consternation were heard from every bean-row.

Clement's nest was really almost more than semi-detached. It had been but lightly wedged between two buttercup stalks. The two eggs in it were at once unseated, and one was broken. Sarah Brown was deeply distressed.

"What a blind fool I am," she said, trying helplessly to replace the nest. "Won't Clement ever come back?"

"Mrs. Clement won't," said the nearest fairy. "She is almost hysterical about the sanctity of the home, and all that. She'll probably get a divorce now."

"Oh, poor Clement, poor Clement," said Sarah Brown. "Will he be terribly cut up?"

"There he is," replied the fairy, pointing upward. "He's watching you. That's Clement's voice you hear."

"Clement's voice," exclaimed Sarah Brown. "Singing like that? Why, he sounds perfectly happy."

"Perfectly happy," mocked the fairy. "His family only sings like that when it's upset. Perfectly happy indeed! Can't you understand tragedy when you hear it?"

Sarah Brown with despairing care tucked the nest up under a bean, and replaced the unbroken egg.

"Do you mean to tell me, then," she said, after a busy painful pause, "that Shelley probably misunderstood that lark he wrote a poem about? He called it a blithe spirit, you know, because it sang. Do you suppose it wasn't one?"

"Certainly not," said the fairy. "I don't know the actual facts of the case, but without a doubt your friend Shelley was standing on the unfortunate bird's nest all the time he was writing his poem."

Sarah Brown, with a deep sigh, began hoeing again.

Fifty beans yet.

She had altogether ceased to find pleasure in the day. Pain is an extinguisher that can put out the sun. She had ceased to find pleasure in the singing of the birds, the voice of the pigeon sounded to her no more than an unbeautiful falsetto growl. She was irritated by the fact that the cuckoo had only one song to sing. She tried not to hoe in time to that song, but the monotony of it possessed her. Her row of beans stretched in front of her right across the world; every time she looked along it the end seemed farther away. Every time she raised her hoe the sword of pain slipped under her guard.

The Dog David, impatient of her unnatural taste in occupations, had forsaken her. She could trace his course by a moving ripple across the potato patch, just as a shark's movement seams the sea.

Forty beans.

Time wears a strangely different guise out of doors. Under the sun time stands almost still. Only when every minute is a physical effort do you discover that there really are sixty minutes in an hour, and that one hour is very little nearer to the evening than another. People who work indoors under the government of clocks never meet time face to face. Their quick seconds are dismissed by the clicking of typewriters, and when their typewriters fall silent, their day is over. We of Out of Doors have a daily eternity to contend with during which only our hands are busy; our minds may grow old and young again between sunrise and sunset; the future may be remade in an hour, hope killed and reborn before a blackbird's song is over. We know the length of days. And after many slow months of stress we come back again, old and bewildered with much silence and much wondering, to our friends in offices, and find them unchanged, floating innocently on the surface of time.

Sarah Brown dropped her hoe and fell upon her knees.

"I can't hoe any more," she said. "There are twenty-five more beans, but I can't hoe them."

"Why should you?" asked the nearest fairy indifferently. "The foreman never notices if we shirk. We always do."

"I said I would hoe this row," said Sarah Brown. "But I am accursed. It is a good thing at least to know one's limitations."

Even in affliction she was prosy.

"I would advise you to go and have your dinner," another fairy said. "Only that I ate your sandwiches as I passed just now. But I left a little lemonade in your bottle. Go under the trees and drink it."

"I can't move," said Sarah Brown.

"Sit there then," said the fairies, and passed on, tickling but not uprooting the weeds in their rows. Fairies are never ill. They have immortal bodies, but no souls. If they see you in pain, they simply think you are flaunting your superiority and your immortal soul in their faces.

The dragon undulated up the field. "Very nicely hoed," he said, looking vaguely at Sarah Brown's row. "Much better than the other rows. Having your dinner? Quite right too."

He never noticed the twenty-five unhoed beans.

Sarah Brown sat on the edge of a shore of green shadow, and a sea of sun speckled with buttercups was before her. David Blessing came and leaned against her. His first intentions were good, he kissed her hurriedly on the chin, but after that he kissed the sandwich bag.

Sarah Brown wondered whether she could cut her throat with a hoe.

"Suicide while of sound mind," she said. "The said mind being entirely sick of its unsound body."

If she sat absolutely still and upright the pain was bearable. But even to think of movement brought tears of pain to her eyes. She detached her mind from her predicament, and sank into a warm tropical sea of thought. She was no real thinker, but she thought much about thinking, and was passionately interested in watching her own mind at work. Thought was like sleep to her, she sank deeply into it without reaching anything profound, nothing resulted but useless dreams, and a certain comforting and defiant intimacy with herself.

She thought of Richard, and wished that she could have hoed a blessing into every bean of his that she had hoed. She noted half-consciously and without surprise that the thought of him was beautiful to her. She could not conjure up his face before her mind, because she always forgot realities, and only remembered dreams. She could not imagine the sound of his voice, she could not recall anything that he had said. Yet she felt again the magic feeling of meeting him, and dreamt of all the things that might have happened, and that might yet happen, yet never would happen, between him and her. All the best things that she remembered had only happened in her dreams, her imagination no sooner sipped the first sip of an experience than it conjured up for her great absurd satisfying draughts of nectar, for which the waking Sarah Brown might thirst in vain. But there was no waking Sarah Brown. Her life was only a sleep-walking; only very rarely did she awake for a moment and feel ashamed to see how alert was the world about her.

So she thought of Richard, not of Richard's Richard, but of some pale private Richard of her own.

The approach of Richard upon a white horse for some time seemed only an extension of her dream. It was only when she realised that he was riding up her bean-row, and partially undoing the work of her hoe, that she awoke suddenly with a start, and caught and tore her breath upon a pin of pain.

It seemed that the afternoon had now long possessed the fields, it had wakened into a live and electric blue the Enchanted Forest which she had last noticed shimmering in its noon green.

All the workers at the approach of Richard were working busily, bent ostentatiously in the form of hairpins up and down their rows. The dragon was rippling anxiously along at the heels of the white horse; a helpless hoping for the best expressed itself in every spike along his spine.

"I don't really know why she's idling like that," Sarah Brown heard him say in his breathy pathetic voice. "I left her hard at work. They're all the same when my back's turned. A fellow needs to have eyes at the tip of his tail."

"Are you suffering from that Leverhulme six-hour-working-day sort of feeling?" asked Richard politely of Sarah Brown, in the manner of an advertisement of a cure for indigestion, as he approached. "I think it's just splendid how receptive and progressive working people are in these days."

"I was meditating suicide," replied Sarah Brown candidly, if faintly. "I am a stricken and useless parasite on the face of your fine earth. But my hoe is too blunt."

"I have a pocket-knife with three blades I could lend you," said Richard, slapping himself enquiringly over several pockets. "Or would you rather try a natty little spell I thought of this morning while I was shaving. I think any one stricken might find it rather useful."

"Ah, give it to me. Give it to me," said Sarah Brown.

The pain was like a wave breaking upon her, carrying her away from her safe shore of shadow, to be lost in seething and suffocating seas without rest. Her eyes felt dried up with fever, and whenever she shut them, the darkness was filled with a jumble of nauseating squares in blue upon a mustard-coloured background. The smell of beans was terrible.

Richard fumbled with something very badly folded up in newspaper. He also tried ineffectively to light a match by wiping it helplessly against his riding breeches. He seemed to have none of the small skill in details that comes to most people before they grow up. He did everything as if he were doing it for the first time.

"I had nothing but the *Morning Post* to wrap it in," he murmured. "I'm afraid that may have spoilt the magic a little."

It was the dragon finally who produced the necessary light. After watching Richard with the anxious sympathy of one ineffectual for another, it said: "Let me," and kindly breathed out a little flame, which set the packet aflare for a moment.

The ashes fluttered down from Richard's hand among the beans, and a thin violet stalk of smoke went up.

Sarah Brown smelt the unmistakable sour smell of magic, and saw soundless words moving Richard's little khaki moustache. Then she found that she had disappeared.

She had never done this before, she had always been present to disturb and interrupt herself. She had never seen the world before, except through the little glazed peepholes, called eyes, through which her everyday self rather wistfully believed that it could see. Now, of course, she knew what seeing was, and for the first time she was aware of the real sizes of things. Poor man measures all things by the size of his own foot. He looks complacently at the print of his boot in the mud, and notices that the ant which he crushed was not nearly as big as his foot, therefore the ant does not matter to him. He also notices that those same feet of his would not be able to walk to the moon within a reasonable time, therefore the moon does not matter to him.

But Sarah Brown had disappeared, and therefore could not measure anything. The spider strode from hill to hill, with the wind rushing through the hair on his back. The blue sky was just a lampshade, clipped on to the earth to shield it from the glare of the gods, beyond it was a mere roof of eternity, pricked with a few billion stars to keep it well ventilated.

Sarah Brown had for a while all the fun of being a god. She was nowhere and she was everywhere. She could have counted the hairs on David's head. The world waved like a flower upon a thin purple stalk of smoke....

Her eyes began to see again. She was aware, of the hollowed tired eyes of Richard fixed upon her. The dragon dawned once more upon her sight, it was inquisitively watching developments, while pretending to claw a weed or two out of a neighbouring bean-row.

The horizon was rusty with a rather heavy sunset. The fields were full of twilight and empty of fairies.

Sarah Brown came to herself with a start, she was shocked to find that she had opened her mouth to say something absolutely impossible to Richard. David's chin was resting on her hand. Her side felt frozen and dangerous but not painful.

"It didn't altogether answer," said Richard. "I'm afraid the wrapping was a mistake. A spell of that strength ought to have set you dancing in three minutes. I'll take you home on my horse. His name is Vivian."

The Horse Vivian, who was so white as to be almost phosphorescent in the dusk, was now further illuminated by a little red light on his breast, and a little green light on his tail. Richard was fond of making elaborate and unnecessary arrangements like this, while neglecting to acquire skill in the more usual handicrafts.

Sarah Brown, a person of little weight, was placed astride on the back of the Horse Vivian. Richard walked beside. The dragon nodded good-bye, and disappeared into its home, a low tunnel-like barn, evidently built specially for it, with a door at each end, and a conveniently placed chimney which enabled it to breathe enough fire to cook its meals without suffocating itself.

Sarah Brown never saw the dragon again, but it stayed always in her memory as a puzzled soul born tragically out of its time, a shorn lamb, so to speak, to whom the wind had not been sufficiently tempered.

Now this ride home, through the Enchanted Forest, on a tall horse, with Richard walking beside her, was the most perfect hour of Sarah Brown's life.

The Enchanted Forest is only an accumulation of dreams, and from every traveller through it it exacts toll in the shape of a dream. By way of receipt, to every traveller it gives a darling memory that neither death nor hell nor paradise can efface.

Sarah Brown knew that her dream and Richard's could never meet. The fact that he was thinking of some one else all the way home was not hidden from her. But she was a person used to living alone, she could enjoy quite lonely romances, and never even envy real women, whose romances were always made for two. She was not a real woman, she was morbidly bodiless. Strange though it may seem, the kind, awkward, absent-minded touch of Richard as he had lifted her on to the Horse Vivian's back had been for her the one flaw in that enchanted ride. She could not bear touch. She had no pleasure in seeing or feeling the skin and homespun that encloses men and women. She hated to watch people feeding themselves, or to see her own thin body in the mirror. She ought really to have been born a poplar tree; a human body was a gift wasted on her.

As they passed along the Green Ride, the red light from the Horse Vivian's neck made a sort of heralding ghost before them on the grass. Bats darted above them for a few yards at a time, and were twitched aside as though by a string or a reminding conscience. The telegraph wires, bound for the post office of Faery, run through the Enchanted Forest, and the poles in the faint light were like tall cruci-fixes. A long way off, through the opening at the end of the Forest, were the little lights of Mitten Island.

"Do you know," said Richard--and this is unfortunately the sort of thing that young men do say at silent and enchanted moments--"that if all the magic in this Forest were collected together and compressed into a liquid form, it would be enough to stop the War in one moment?"

"My hat!" said Sarah Brown. "In one moment?"

"In one moment."

"My hat!" said Sarah Brown.

"The powers of magic haven't been anything like thoroughly estimated even yet," said Richard.

"I suppose the War was made by black magic," suggested Sarah Brown, trying to talk intelligently and to be faithful to her own thoughts at the same time.

"Good Lord, no," replied Richard. "The worst of this war is that it has noth-ing whatever to do with magic of any sort. It was made and is supported by men who had forgotten magic, it is the result of the coming to an end of a spell. Haven't you noticed that a spell came to an end at the beginning of the last century? Why, doesn't almost every one see something lacking about the Victorian age?"

"Something certainly died with Keats and Shelley," sighed Sarah Brown.

"Oh well," said Richard, "I don't know about books. I can't read, you know. But obviously what was wrong with the last century was just that it didn't believe in fairies."

"Does this century believe in fairies? If the spell came to an end, how is it that we are so magic now?"

"This century knows that it doesn't know everything," said Richard. "And as for spells--we have started a new spell. That's the curious part of this War. So gross and so impossible and so unmagic was its cause, that magic, which had been virtual-ly dead, rose again to meet it. The worse a world grows, the greater will magic grow to save it. Magic only dies in a tepid world. I think there is now more magic in the world than ever before. The soil of France is alive with it, and as for Belgium--when Belgium gets back home at last she will find her desecrated house enchanted.... And the same applies to all the thresholds in the world which fighting-men have crossed and will never cross again, except in the dreams of their friends. That sort of austere and secret magic, like a word known by all and spoken by none, is pretty nearly all that is left to keep the world alive now...."

Richard seemed to be becoming less and less of a man and more and more of a wizard the farther he penetrated into the Enchanted Forest. He was saying things that would have embarrassed him very much had they been said in the Piccadilly Restaurant, even after three glasses of champagne. For this reason, although the borders of the Enchanted Forest are said to be widening, it is to be hoped that they will not encroach beyond the confines of the Parish of Faery. What would happen if its trees began to seed themselves in the Strand? Imagine the Stock Exchange under the shadow of an enchanted oak, and the consequent disastrous wearing thin of the metal casing in which all good business men keep their souls.

Sarah Brown thought if rather a curious coincidence that so soon after they had spoken of the dead Keats they should see him alive. They saw him framed in a little pale aisle of the Forest, a faintly defined fragile ghost, crouched against the trunk of a tree, bent awkwardly into an attitude of pain forgotten and ecstatic attention. It was his dearest moment that they saw, a moment without death. For he was a prisoner in a perfect spell; he was utterly entangled in the looped and ensnaring song of a nightingale. The song was like beaten gold wire. Never again in her life did Sarah Brown profane with her poor voice the words that a perfect singer begot in a marriage with a perfect song. But in unhappiness, and in the horrible nights, the song came to her, always....

The travellers were approaching the end of the Green Ride, but that did not matter to Sarah Brown, for there had been nothing lacking all the way.

"Love----," began Richard in a loud exalted voice, and then suddenly a search-light glared diagonally across the end of the Ride, over Mitten Island, and quenched the magic of the moment.

"Sorry," said Richard. "I thought I was talking to my True Love."

"I'm sorry you weren't," said Sarah Brown, as they emerged from the Forest. "I mean, I'm sorry it was only me you were talking to."

CHAPTER VIII
THE REGRETTABLE WEDNESDAY

What a very singular thing," said the Mayor, meeting the witch towards three o'clock in the afternoon, as she came down the Broad Walk towards Kensington, having slept invisibly among the daffodils for nearly twelve hours. "A really very singular thing. 'Tisn't once in five years I visit these parts, and now I'm here I meet the very person I was thinkin' about." He winked.

"It's almost like magic, isn't it," said the witch, winking busily in return.

"Well, I've done what you told me to," said the Mayor.

"What was that?"

"You will 'ave your joke," he retorted indulgently. "Pretending not to know, indeed. I've done what you told me the other day when you came to that committee with your cat. I thought it over--I'm not a proud man, never above takin' a hint,-- and I admitted to meself that what you said was fair about makin' money. Some'ow I never thought but what money was the first thing to make in business. To tell you the truth, I always thought it rather a feather in my cap that I never took advantage of Brown Borough customers in selling adulterated goods, for--Lawdy--they'd swallow anythink. It's different with your business, bein' in an 'igher-class locality. 'Igh prices, I thought, was only natural. Make 'ay while the sun shines was my motter, and I says to meself there was no reason why this war should make *everyone* un'appy. As for lookin' at the grocery business as a trust from God, like you said, I never dremp of such a thing, although I've bin to Chapel regular for ten years. But I see now there was a lot in what you said, and when I come to think of it, there was no need to make such a terrible lot of extra hay, 'owever much the sun might be shinin'. When you put it like that, I couldn't say why I was so set on more money, 'aving quite enough. Well, I says to meself, after shutting meself up to think it out, like you said, 'ere am I giving up all my life an' all my jolly days an' 'olidays, an' I'm damned if I know what for. For money,--just money stewin' in its own juice in a bank,--not money I can use. Well, everybody's trained so, I'm thinkin'. Anyway I took it friendly of you to put it so delicate, so fanciful as you did, so as them charity ladies didn't smell a rat. I appreciated that, an' thought the more of what you said. I'm not a proud man."

"You're just proud enough," said the witch. "You're a darling. If ever I can help you in a business way, let me know. If you want to start a side line, for instance, in Happiness, I can give you a tip where to get it wholesale, within limits. It'd go like wildfire in the Brown Borough, if you put in an ounce or two, gratis of course, with every order."

"You will 'ave your joke," murmured the Mayor. "But I like it in you. I'm a man that never takes a joke amiss. Let's go for a walk together."

"No," said the witch. "I am so hungry that my ribs are beginning to bend in-wards. I must go and have sausages and mash and two apple dumplings."

They found themselves presently seated at the marble-topped table of an A.B.C. After an interval that could hardly be accurately described as presently, sausages and mash dawned on the horizon, and the witch waved her fork rudely at it as it approached.

"Mashed is splendid stuff to sculp with," she said, roughing in a ground plan upon her plate with the sure carelessness of the artist. "This is going to be an ivory castle built upon a rock in a glassy sea. The sausage is the dragon guarding it, and this little crumb of bread is the emprisoned princess, a dull but sterling creature----"

"Look 'ere, Miss Watkins," interrupted the Mayor. "I'm not as a rule an impul-sive man, and I don't want to startle you----"

"How d'you mean startle me?" asked the witch. "You haven't startled me at all. But the fact is, I never have been much of a person for getting married, thank you very much. I'm an awful bad house-keeper. And I *do* so much enjoy having no money."

"Well, I'm blessed," exclaimed the Mayor. "You're a perfect witch, I declare." He laid a large meat-like hand upon hers. "But you know, you can't put the lid on me so easy as that. Ever since you came into that old committee room I saw there was something particular about you, something that you an' me 'ad in common. I'm not speakin' so much of us bein' in the same line of business. Some'ow--oh, 'ang it all, let's get out of this and take a taxi. I'm not a kissing man, but----"

He seemed very persistent in applying negatived adjectives to himself. It was not his fault if the world failed to grasp exactly what he was, or rather exactly what he was not.

"I have often wondered," interrupted the witch, "talking of kissing--what would happen if two snipes wanted to kiss each other? It would have to be at such awfully long range, wouldn't it. Or----"

"Come off it," ordered the Mayor irritably. "What about gettin' out of this and----"

"Don't you think this is becoming rather a tiresome scene?" said the witch. "Somehow over luscious, don't you think? I wish those apple dumplings would hurry up."

"'Ere, miss," said the Mayor ungraciously to a passing whirlwind. "'Urry them dumplings."

"'Urry them dumplings," echoed the whirlwind to a little hole in the wall.

The witch had a silly vision of two distressed dumplings, like dilatory chorus girls, mad with the nightmare feeling of not being dressed in time, hearing their cue called in a heartless voice from the inexorable sky, desperately applying the last dab of flour to their imperfect complexions. But the witch found no fault with them when they came. She gave them her whole attention for some minutes.

"Well, well," she said, laying down her fork and spoon, "that's good. I feel awfully grown-up, having had a proposal. When real girls ask me now how many I've had, I shall be able to say One. But I met a girl the other day who had had six. She had six photographs, but she called them scalps. If you would give me your photograph I could label it A Scalp, and hang it in the Shop. That would be very grown-up, wouldn't it?"

"You will 'ave your joke," said the Mayor in a hollow voice. "I never met such a gurl as you for a bit of fun. I don't believe you've got any 'eart."

There, of course, he was right. A heart is a sort of degree conferred by Providence on those who have passed a certain examination. Magic people are only freshmen in our college, and it is useless for us--secure in the possession of many learned letters after our names--to despise them. They will become sophisticated in due course.

"How d'you mean--heart?" asked the witch therefore. "I've still got an awful hunger inside me, if that's anything to do with it. I'll tell you what. It's Wednesday. Let's go and call on Miss Ford. She might have grassy sandwiches."

There was a most abrupt and disturbing draught in Miss Ford's sleek and decorous flat as the witch and the Mayor entered it. The serenity of the night and the morning had been suddenly obliterated, and Kensington suffered a gust or two of gritty wind which blew the babies home from the Gardens, and kept all the window-gazers in the High Street on the alert with their fingers on the triggers of their umbrellas.

But no rain fell. Rain cannot fall in this book of fine weather.

The draught that intruded into the flat ruffled the neat hair of five persons, Miss Ford herself, Lady Arabel Higgins, Miss Ivy MacBee, Mr. Bernard Tovey, and Mr. Darnby Frere.

Miss MacBee always seemed to be seated on tenterhooks, even in the most comfortable of chairs. Her Spartan spine never consented graciously to the curves of cushions. She had smooth padded hair and smooth padded manners, and her eyes were magnified by thick pince-nez to a cow-like size. Most people, especially most women, were instinctively sorry for her, because she always looked a little clever and very uncomfortable.

Mr. Bernard Tovey was a blunt-nosed beaming person. He leaned forward abruptly whenever he spoke, thereby swinging a lock of hair into his right eye. He agreed so heartily with everything that was said that people who addressed him were left with the happy impression that they had said something Rather Good. This habit, combined with the fact that he never launched an independent remark, had given him the reputation of being one of the best talkers in Kensington.

Mr. Darnby Frere was the editor of an advanced religious paper called *I Wonder*, but he never wondered really. He knew almost everything, and therefore, while despising the public for knowing so little, he encouraged it to continue wondering, so that he might continue despising and instructing it.

Now it was an almost unprecedented thing for two members of the small trades-man class to come into Miss Ford's drawing-room, especially on a Wednesday. The utmost social mingling of the classes that those walls had ever seen was the moment when Miss Ford asked the electric light man what he thought of the war. The electric light man's reply had been quoted in the dialect on two or three of the following Wednesdays, as a proof of Miss Ford's daring intimacy with men in Another Station of Life. Really it would have been simpler, though of course not so picturesque, to have quoted it direct from its original source, ***John Bull***, the electric light man's Bible.

The entrance of the witch and the Mayor was to a certain extent a crisis, but Miss Ford kept her head, and her three friends, though grasping at once the extraordinary situation, did not give way to panic.

"Well, well, well," said the Mayor, looking round and breathing very loudly. "This is a cosy little nook you've got 'ere."

He was not at all at his ease, but being a business man, and being also blessed with a peculiarly inexpressive face, he was successfully dissembling his discomfort.

For it had happened that the lift had been one of those lifts that can do no wrong, the kind that the public is indulgently allowed to work by itself. And the Mayor, looking upon this fact as specially planned by a propitious god of love, had tried to kiss the witch as they shot up the darkened shaft. If I remind you that the witch was still accompanied by her broomstick, Harold, a creature of unreasoning fidelity, I need hardly describe the scene further. The Mayor stepped out of the lift with a tingling scraped face, and if he had possessed enough hair on his head, it would have been on end. As it was, when the lift stopped, he retrieved his hat from the floor with a frank oath, and, as the witch had at once rung the bell of Miss Ford's flat, he instinctively followed her across that threshold.

She looked round in the hall, and said with a friendly smile: "I'm afraid Harold gets a bit irritable sometimes. I often tell him to count ten before he lets himself go, but he forgets. Did he hurt you?"

I am afraid the angry Mayor did not give Harold credit for much initiative.

"Kissing is such a funny habit, isn't it," said the witch briskly as she shook Miss Ford's hand. "I wonder who decided in the first place which forms of contact should express which forms of emotion. I wonder----"

She interrupted herself as her eyes fell on some green sandwiches which were occupying the third floor of a wicker Eiffel Tower beside Miss Ford. "Oh how gorgeous," she said. "Do you know, I've only had two meals in the last two days."

Nobody present had ever been obliged to miss a meal, so this statement seemed to every one to be a message from another world.

"You must tell us about all your experiences, my dear Miss Watkins," said Miss Ford, leading the witch towards a chair by the fire. The witch sat down suddenly cross-legged on the hearth-rug, leaving her rather embarrassed hostess in the air, so to speak, towering rigidly above her.

"How d'you mean--experiences?" said the witch, after eating one sandwich in silent ecstasy. "I was up in the sky last night, talking to a German. Was that an experience?"

"The sky last night was surely no place for a lady," said Mr. Frere with rather sour joviality.

"Oh, I know what she means," said Miss MacBee earnestly. "I was up in the sky last night too----"

"Great Scott," exclaimed the witch. "But----"

"Yes, I was," persisted Miss MacBee. "I lay on the hammock which I have had slung in my cellar, and shut my eyes, and loosed my spirit, and it shot upward like a lark released. It detached itself from the common trammels of the body, yes, my spirit, in shining armour, fought with the false, cruel spirits of murderers."

"I hadn't got any shining armour," sighed the witch, who had been looking a little puzzled. "But I had the hell of a wrangle with a Boche witch who came over. We fought till we fell off our broomsticks, and then she quoted the *Daily Mail* at me, and then she fell through a hole and broke her back over the cross on St. Paul's."

It was Miss MacBee's turn to look puzzled, but she said to Miss Ford: "My dear, you have brought us a real mystic."

Mr. Frere, though emitting an applauding murmur, leaned back and fixed his face in the ambiguous expression of one who, while listening with interest to the conversation of liars, is determined not to appear deceived.

"How d'you mean--mystic?" asked the witch. "I don't think I can have made myself clear. Excuse me," she added to Miss Ford, "but this room smells awfully clever to any one coming in from outside. Do you mind if I dance a little, to move the air about?"

"We shall be delighted," said Miss Ford indulgently. "Shall I play for you?"

The witch did not answer; she rose, and as she rose she threw a little white pa-per packet into the fire. She danced round the sofa and the chairs. The floor shook a little, and all her watchers twisted their necks gravely, like lizards watching an active fly.

The parlour-maid, by appearing in the doorway with an inaudible announce-ment, diverted their attention, though she did not interrupt the witch's exercises.

A very respectable-looking man came in. Darnby Frere, who was a student of Henry James's works, and therefore constantly made elaborate guesses on mat-ters that did not concern him, and then forgot them because--unlike Mr. James's guesses--they were always wrong, gave the newcomer credit for being perhaps a shopwalker, or perhaps a South-Eastern and Chatham ticket-collector, but surely a chapel-goer.

At any rate the stranger looked ill at ease, and especially disconcerted by the sight of the dancing witch.

Miss Ford realised by now that her Wednesday had for some reason gone mad. She had lost her hold on the reins of that usually dignified equipage; there was nothing now for her to do but to grip tight and keep her head.

She therefore concealed her ignorance of her newest guest's identity, she stiff-ened her lips and poured out another cup of tea with a nerveless hand. The stranger took the cup of tea with some relief, and said: "Thenk you, meddem."

The witch stopped dancing, and stood in front of the newcomer's chair.

"I think yours must be a discouraging job," she said to him. "Getting people punished for doing things you'd love to do yourself. Oh, awfully discouraging. And do tell me, there's a little problem that's been on my mind ever since the war start-ed. I hear that Hindenburg says the German Army intends to march through Lon-don the moment it can brush away the obstacles in front of it. Have you considered what will happen to the traffic, because you know Germans on principle march on the wrong side of the street--indeed everybody in the world does, except the conscientious British. Think of the knotted convulsions of traffic at the Bank, with a hundred thousand Boches goose-stepping on the wrong side of the road--think of poor thin Fleet Street, and the dam that would occur in Piccadilly Circus. What do you policemen intend to do about it?"

"I don't know I'm sure, miss," said the newcomer coldly. "It's a long time since I was on point duty. I'm a plain clothes man, meddem," he added to Miss Ford. "I'm afraid I'm intruding on your tea-party, owing to your maid misunderstanding my business. But being 'ere, I 'ope you'll excuse me stating what I've come for."

"Oh certainly, certainly," said Miss Ford, who was staring vaguely into the fireplace. A rather fascinating thread of lilac smoke was spinning itself out of the ashes of the little white paper packet.

"The names of the Mayor of the Brown Borough, Miss Meter Mostyn Ford, and Lady A. 'Iggins--all of 'oom I understand from the maid are present--'ave been mentioned as being presoomably willing to give information likely to be 'elpful in the search for a suspicious cherecter 'oo is believed to 'ave intruded on a cheritable meeting, at which you were present last Seturday, in order to escape arrest, 'aving just perpetrated a petty theft from a baker, 'Ermann Schwab. The cherecter is charged now with a more important offence, being in possession of an armed flying machine, in defiance of the Defence of the Realm Act, and interfering with the work of 'Is Majesty's Forces during enemy attack. The cherecter is believed to be a man in female disguise, but enquiry up to date 'as failed to get any useful description. You ladies and gents, I understand, should be able to 'elp the Law in this metter."

There was a stunned silence in the room, broken only by the pastoral sound of the witch eating grassy sandwiches. After a moment Miss Ford, the Mayor, and Lady Arabel all began speaking at once, and each stopped with a look of relief on hearing that some one else was ready to take the responsibility of speaking.

Then the witch began with her mouth full: "You know----," but Lady Arabel interrupted her.

"Angela dear, be silent. This does not concern you. Of course, inspector, we're all only too dretfully anxious to do anything to help the Law, but you must specify the occasion more exactly. Our committee sees so many applicants."

"You are Lady A. 'Iggins, I believe," said the policeman impassively. "Well, my lady, may I ask you whether you are aware thet the cherecter in question was seen to leave your 'ouse last night, at nine forty-five P.M., after the warning of approaching enemy atteck was given, and to disappear in an easterly direction, on a miniature 'eavier than air machine, make and number unknown?"

The threads of curious smoke in the fireplace were increasing. They shivered as though with laughter, and flowed like crimped hair up the chimney.

"I had a dinner-party last night certainly," stammered Lady Arabel. A trembling seized the sock she was knitting. She had turned the heel some time ago, but in the present stress had forgotten all about the toe. The prolonged sock grew every minute more and more like a drain-pipe with a bend in it. "Why yes, of course I had a dinner-party; why shouldn't I? My son Rrchud, a private in the London Rifles, this young lady, Miss Angela--er--, and her friend--such a good quiet creature...."

"And 'oo else was in the 'ouse?" asked the policeman, glancing haughtily at the witch.

"Oh nobody, nobody. The servants all gave notice and left--too dretfully tahsome how they can't stand Rrchud and his ways. Of course there was the orchestra--twenty-five pieces--but *so* dependable."

"Dependable," said the witch, "is a mystery word to me. I can't think how it got into the English language without being right. Surely Depend-on-able----"

"Your son 'as peculiar ways, you say, my lady," interrupted the policeman.

"Oh, nothing to speak of," answered Lady Arabel, wincing. "Merely lighthearted ... too dretfully Bohemian ... ingenious, you know, in making experiments ... magnetism...."

"Experiments in Magnetism," spelt the policeman aloud into his notebook. "And 'oo left your 'ouse at nine forty-five P.M. last night?"

"I did," said the witch.

The policeman withered her once more with a glance.

"Lady 'Iggins, did you say your son left your 'ouse at nine forty-five P.M. last night?"

"Yes, but----"

"Thenk you, my lady."

"You seem to me dretfully impertinent," said Lady Arabel. "This is not a court of law. My son Rrchud left the house with me and our guest to seek shelter from the raid."

"Thenk you, my lady," repeated the policeman coldly, and turned to Miss Ford.

"Could you identify the cherecter 'oo came into your committee room last Seturday?" he asked of her.

"No," she replied.

"Couldn't you say whether it seemed like a male or a female in disguise? Couldn't you mention any physical pecooliarity that struck you?"

"No," said Miss Ford.

"'Ave you no memory of last Seturday night?"

"No," said Miss Ford.

"I have," said the witch.

The policeman bridled. "I was addressing this 'ere lady, Miss M.M. Ford. Can you at least tell me, meddem, 'ow long you and the 'Iggins family 'ave been acquainted?"

"No," said Miss Ford.

"Eighteen years," said Lady Arabel.

The fumes from the fireplace were very strong indeed, but nobody called attention to them.

"I'm sorry, ..." said Miss Ford presently, very slowly, "that ... I ... can't help you. I have ... been having ... nerve-storms ... since ... last ... Saturday...."

The policeman fixed his ominous gaze upon her for quite a minute before he wrote something in his notebook.

"Is Private Richard 'Iggins in town to-night?" he asked of Lady Arabel in a casual voice.

"I suppose so," she replied. "But he has such a dretful habit of disappearing...."

The policeman turned to the Mayor.

"Now, sir," he said. "Could you help me at all in----"

"Look here," said the witch, rising. "If you would only come along to my house in Mitten Island I can truly give you all the information you need. In fact, won't you come to supper with me? If some one will kindly lend me half a crown I will go on ahead and cook something."

Mr. Tovey mechanically produced a coin.

"Here, Harold," called the witch, and holding Harold's collar she stepped out on to the balcony, mounted, and flew away.

She left a room full of noise behind her.

The policeman, who was intoxicated with the strange fumes, said: "Hell. Hell.

Hell."

Lady Arabel called in vain: "Angela, Angela, don't be so dretfully rash."

Mr. Tovey, now afflicted with a lock of hair in each eye, seized the policeman by the shoulder thinking to prevent him from jumping out of the window. "You fool," he shouted.

The Mayor slapped his thigh with a loud report. "Lawdy," he yelled. "She's a sport. She will 'ave 'er joke."

Miss MacBee laughed hysterically and very loudly.

Mr. Darnby Frere said "My word" rather cautiously several times, and rubbed the bridge of his nose. He rather thought everybody was pulling his leg, but could not be sure.

Only Miss Ford sat silent.

CHAPTER IX
THE HOUSE OF LIVING ALONE MOVES AWAY

When Sarah Brown and Richard, followed by the Dog David, reached the Mitten Island Ferry, after travelling slowly by moonlight, they were surprised to see a great crowd of people banked up on the Island, and one man in the uniform of a policeman, standing alone on the mainland. About ten yards from land the ferryman sat in his boat, rowing gently to keep himself stationary in the current.

"You'll 'ave to come to shore now," said the policeman, in the tone of one exhausted by long argument. "'Ere's some more parties wanting to cross." He turned to Richard. "Look 'ere, mate," he said. "I'm 'ere in the discharge of my dooty, and this ferryman is obstructin' me."

"Deah, deah," said Richard.

The ferryman said: "If the King of England--why, if the two ghosts of Queen Victoria and Albert the Good--was waiting to cross now, I wouldn't come in for them, not if it was going to give you a chance to set foot on Mitten Island."

The crowd across the river, divining that a climax of defiance was being reached, shouted: "Yah, yah," in unison.

"Is either of you parties an 'ouse'older on Mitten Island?" asked the policeman of Sarah Brown and Richard.

"I am," said Richard, to his companion's surprise.

"Can you give me any information regarding the whereabouts of a cherecter known under any of these names: Iris 'Yde, T.B. Watkins, Hangela the Witch, possibly a male in female disguise, believed to conduct a general shop and boardin' 'ouse on Mitten Island?"

"There is only one shop on Mitten Island," said Richard. "And one boarding house. All in one. I own it. I can recite you the prospectus if you like. I have a superintendent there. I have known her all my life. I did not know she was believed to be a male in female disguise. I did not know she had any name at all, let alone half-a-dozen."

The policeman seemed to be troubled all the time by mosquitoes. He slapped his face and his ears and the back of his neck. He succeeded in killing one insect upon the bridge of his nose, and left it there by mistake, a strangely ignoble corpse. Sarah Brown suspected Richard of some responsibility for this untimely persecution.

"That party is charged with an offence against the Defence of the Realm Act," said the policeman,--"with being, although a civilian, in possession of a flying machine, and--er--obstructin' 'Is Majesty's enemies in the performance of their dooty."

"Oh deah, deah," said Richard. "Deah, deah, deah...."

"Do either of you know the present whereabouts of the party?" persisted the policeman. Attacked on every side by insects, he was becoming rather pathetic in his discomfort and indignity. His small eyes, set in red fat, stared with uncomprehending protest; his fat busy hands were not agile enough to defend him. He felt unsuccessful and foolish, and very near the ground. He wished quite disproportionately to be at home with his admiring wife in Acton.

Sarah Brown shook her head in reply, and Richard could say nothing but "Oh deah, deah...."

"May I take your name and 'ome address, and regimental number, please, young man," said the policeman, after a baffled pause.

"Now my address," said Richard, with genuine shame, "is a thing I honestly can never remember. I know I've heard it; I've tried and tried to learn it at my mother's knee. It begins with an H, I think. That's the worst of not being able to read or write. I can describe the place to you exactly, a house with a lot of windows, that sees a long way. If you turn your back on the Marble Arch, and go on till you get to a big poster saying Eat Less Meat, and then turn to your right--(pointing to the left)--or again, if you go by air as the crow flies--or rather as the witch flies----"

"You shall 'ear of this foolery, my fine feller," said the distressed policeman, almost with a break in his voice. "Seein' as 'ow you refuse information, an' this ferryman thinks fit to defy the law, I 'ave no course open but to whistle for my mate, and leave 'im 'ere while I telephone for a police-boat."

He raised his whistle to his lips, but before he could blow it, the climax of this the least successful evening of his life, overwhelmed him. A shadow swept over the party, a large flying substance caught him full on the back of the neck and knocked him off the landing-stage into the river.

The witch on Harold her Broomstick landed on the spot vacated by the policeman.

"Oh, look what I've done, look what I've done ..." she exclaimed in an ecstasy of vexation. There was no need to tell anybody to look. Five hundred odd people were already doing so with enthusiasm. "Oh, what a dreadfully bad landing! Oh, Harold, how could you be so careless?"

She took the cringing Harold by the mane and slapped him violently once or twice. Richard stretched out his riding-crop to the splashing policeman, murmuring: "Oh deah, deah...."

"Don't be frightened," said the witch to the policeman. "We'll soon get you out, and the water's so shallow you can't sink. Talking of sinking, Richard, there's a question that puzzles me rather. If a rat got on to a submarine, how would it behave? A submarine, you see, is a sinking ship, and rats pride themselves so on knowing when to----"

Sarah Brown seized the witch by the shoulder. "Go away, witch," she said.

"How d'you mean--go away?" asked the witch. "I've only just this minute come."

"Go away, go away," was all that Sarah Brown could manage to repeat.

"Oh, very well," said the witch in her offended grown-up voice. "I can take a hint, I suppose, as well as anybody. I'm going."

She seated herself with an irritable flouncing movement on Harold's saddle, and flew away.

The policeman climbed out of the water, looking like an enraged seal. Peals of laughter from the other side of the moonlit river robbed him of adequate words.

"Not ser fast, my fine feller," he roared, seeing Richard kissing the Horse Vivian on the nose, preparatory to riding away. "Don't you think for a minute I don't know 'oo's at the bottom of this."

"You don't know how tired I am of loud noises," said Richard, lifting one foot with dignity to the stirrup. "You don't know how bitterly I long to be still and hear things very far off ... but always there is an angry voice or the angry noise of guns in the way...."

He twined one finger negligently into the mane on the Horse Vivian's neck, and pulled himself slowly into the saddle. The policeman stood mysteriously impotent. Water dripped loudly from his clothes and punctuated Richard's quiet speech.

"Dear policeman," continued Richard. "I believe you have talked so much to-night that you haven't heard what a quiet night it is. You are smaller than a star, and yet you make more noise than all the stars together. You are not so cold as the moon, and yet your teeth chatter more loudly than hers. The heat of your wrath is less than the heat of the sun, and yet, while he is silent and departed, you fill the air with clamour, and--if I may say so--seem to be outstaying your welcome. Oh, dear policeman, listen.... Do you know, if there were no London on this side and no War on that, the silence would be deep enough to fill all the seas of all the worlds...."

He shook the reins, and the Horse Vivian moved, treading quietly on the strip of grass that borders the path to the ferry.

"I am going to talk to my True Love now," said Richard, his voice fading away as he rode. "My True Love's voice is the only voice that is a little more beautiful to me than silence...."

For a moment he looked every inch a wizard. Every button on his uniform and every buckle on the Horse Vivian's harness caught the moonlight, and changed into faery spangles as he turned and waved his hand before disappearing.

The policeman seemed quieted, as he looked at Sarah Brown sitting, white and haggard with pain, on the river bank, with her arm round the shivering David.

"In a minute, in a minute, my One," she was saying to David. "We are nearly home now. We shall soon be quiet now."

There was always something startlingly inoffensive about Sarah Brown's appearance.

"I'd like to know 'oo was responsible for this houtrage, all the same," said the policeman.

Sarah Brown did not hear him, but she said: "Oh, I am so very sorry it happened. It was a pure accident, of course, but it is so terrible to see any one have an accident to his dignity. You must forget it quickly, you must run and find someone who knows you at your best, you must tell her a fine revised version of the incident, and then you will feel better."

The ferryman shouted: "I don't mind coming in now to fetch this young woman. You can come too now if you like, Mr. Pompous-in-the-Pond, for the party you're looking for is not at home, and I've no doubt but what that crowd over there will give you a gay welcome."

"I'll look into the metter to-morrer," said the policeman. "You 'aven't 'eard the last of this, none of you 'aven't, not by a long chalk. I've a good mind to get the Mayor to read the Riot Act at you."

As Sarah Brown landed on Mitten Island she could not distinguish the faces of the waiting crowd, but she heard sharp anxious voices.

"They ain't goin' to get 'er, not if I knows it."

"She never speaks but kindness, the dear lamb."

"She's more of a saint than any in the Calendar."

"She gave my Danny a room in 'er house, and put 'eart into 'im after 'e lost 'is sight in the War."

"She's the good fairy of the Island."

"She grew all them Sweet Williams in my garden in one night, when I first come 'ere and was 'omesick for Devon."

"The law's always after saints and fairies, always 'as bin."

"But the law can't catch 'er."

"The law has driven her away," said Sarah Brown. "There is no magic now on Mitten Island."

She staggered through the open door of the Shop. "This is Richard's house," she said to herself as she entered, and felt doubly alone because Richard was far away, riding to his True Love. She struck her last match, lit the lantern, and looked round. There was no sound in the house of Living Alone, she thought there would never again be any magic sound there to penetrate to her imprisoned hearing. The aprons hanging from the ceiling near the door flapped in the cold wind, and she thought they were like grey bats in a cave. The breeze blew out the open lantern. Ah, how desolate, how desolate....

A piece of paper was impaled upon the counter by means of a headless hatpin.

There was something very largely and badly written on it. Sarah Brown read: "Well Soup it looks like my Night's come and what dyou think Sherry's come too. Im an me as gone off to a place e knows that's a fine place for such a boy as Elbert to be born in so no more at present from your true Peony."

Sarah Brown climbed up the short stairway, painful step by painful step, to her cell. She sat on her bed holding her throbbing side, and breathing with fearful caution. She looked at the empty grate. She put a cigarette in her mouth, the unconscious and futile answer of the Dweller Alone to that blind hunger for comfort. But she had no matches, and presently, dimly conscious that her groping for comfort had lacked result, she absently put another cigarette into her mouth, and then felt a fool.

She stared at the cold window. The sky seemed to be nailed carelessly to it by means of a crooked star or two.

These are the terrible nights of Living Alone, when you have fever and sometimes think that your beloved stands in the doorway to bring you comfort, and sometimes think that you have no beloved, and that there is no one left in all the world, no word, no warmth, nor ever a kindly candle to be lighted in that spotted darkness that walls up your hot sight. Again on those nights you dream that you have already done those genial things your body cries for, or perhaps That Other has done them. The fire is built and alight at last, a cup of something cool and beautifully sour stands ready to your hand, you can hear the delicious rattle of china on a tray in the passage--someone coming with food you would love to look at, and presently perhaps to eat ... when you feel better. But again and again your eyes open on the cold dumb darkness, and there is nothing but the wind and strange sinister emptiness creaking on the stair.

These are the terrible nights of Living Alone, yet no real lover of that house and of that state would ever exchange one of those haunted and desert nights for a night spent watched, in soft warm places.

Sarah Brown was not long left alone that night to look at the strip of moonlight on the cold ashes of her fireplace. The Shop below shook suddenly with many footfalls, and the metallic officious barking of the Dog David rent the still air of her cell.

A man's voice at the foot of the stairs said: "I can hear a dog barking." And a woman's voice followed it: "Angela, dear, is that you?"

Sarah Brown was only aware of a vague and irksome disturbance. She groped to her door, opened it, and shouted miserably: "Go away, policeman, go away. She is not here."

Lady Arabel came up, flashing an electric torch.

"My dear, you look dretfully ill. Why look, you are trembling. Why look, your little dog is making your counterpane muddy. Don't be afraid for Angela, we are all here to try and help her."

"All here?"

"Yes, Meta and the Mayor and Mr. Tovey and Mr. Frere. Let me help you into bed, and then you shall tell me what you know of her. You have had a dretfully trying time."

"I am well," said Sarah Brown ungraciously. "You are none of you going to help the witch without me."

"Ah, this is all very dretful," sighed Lady Arabel. "Most foolish of us to come here all together like this, after the policeman took our names and addresses, and was dretfully impertinent and suspicious. But Meta insisted. I quite expect to spend the next twenty-four hours in gaol, or else to be shot for Offence of the Realm. In fact, speaking as a ratepayer, I think the police ought to have done it before. Still, Meta thought we might perhaps be able to help Angela.... Meta has many friends who seem influential ... but *so* talkative, my dear."

She led the way downstairs. Mr. Tovey and the Mayor were talking at the foot of the stairs, Mr. Frere was listening sardonically. As Sarah Brown went past them into the Shop, she smelt the unflower-like scent that always denoted the presence of Miss Ford. Sarah Brown herself was accompanied by nothing more seductive than a faint smell of gasoline, showing that her clothes had lately been home-cleaned. In the darkness of the Shop she saw Miss Ford stooping, trying to shut the big difficult drawer in which the witch kept her magic.

"It is frightfully explosive," said Sarah Brown.

Miss Ford started and straightened her back. "Ah, Miss Brown.... I was just looking about...."

Sarah Brown sat gasping on the counter, and the rest of the party re-entered the Shop, bringing the lantern.

"How very absurd all this is," said Miss Ford nervously,--"taking such a great deal of trouble about a necessitous case."

"America is in my mind," said Lady Arabel. "If we could get her there. Anybody who has done anything silly goes to America. Indeed, if I remember rightly, America is entirely populated with fugitives from somewhere else. So dretfully confusing for the Red Indians. They say the story of the Tower of Babel was only a prophecy about the Woolworth Building--"

"You couldn't get a passport," said Mr. Darnby Frere, who was the only person present really conscious of sanity. "Only a miracle could produce a passport in these days, especially for a fugitive from justice."

"Only a miracle--or magic," said Sarah Brown.

Miss Ford moved instinctively behind the counter towards the open drawer full of ingredients for happiness.

"We must remember," added Mr. Frere, "that, after all, she did break the law. In fact I cannot for the life of me imagine why on earth we are all--"

"Oh, Darnby, do be sensible," said Miss Ford. "Of course we know it is wrong to break the law, but in this case--well, I myself should be the last to blame her."

"No, not the last," said Sarah Brown.

"What do you mean?"

"Certainly not the last. Probably not even the penultimate one. You flatter yourself."

"Why, surely some of you ladies, movin' in the 'ighest circles, knows of gentlemen in the Foreign Office that would do a little shut-eye job, for old times' sake," suggested the Mayor.

This was a challenge to Miss Ford. She ceased to gaze haughtily on Sarah Brown. "Men from three departments of the Foreign Office are fairly regular Wednesday friends of mine," she said. "But I could hardly trouble any of them on--er--so trivial a matter."

There was silence, while Miss Ford toyed gingerly with one of the paper packets out of the witch's drawer. Presently she said: "What about Richard?"

Lady Arabel showed sudden irritation. "There you go again, Meta; I have spoken to you of it again and again. It's Rrchud this and Rrchud that whenever anything in the least tahsome or out of the way happens. One would think you considered the poor boy a wizard."

"You needn't lose your temper, Arabel," said Miss Ford coldly. "I only meant that Richard might be useful, having so many friends, and such skill in ... chemistry...." As if unconsciously she tore off one corner of the packet of magic she held before adding: "And besides, as I have often told you, I believe Richard to have real Occult Power, which would give him a special interest in this case."

Sarah Brown, who was burying her face in her hands and missing much of the conversation, caught the name of Richard, and said: "Richard has gone to his True Love."

A tempest of restrained embarrassment arose.

"She's feverish," murmured Miss Ford, turning scarlet.

"My dear Sarah," said Lady Arabel tartly. "You are quite mistaken, and I must beg of you to be careful how you repeat idle gossip about my son. Rrchud is at his office. You know it is only open at night--one of Rrchud's quaint fancies."

"I will ring up his office," said Miss Ford, deciding to ignore Sarah Brown both now and in future. "Where is the telephone?"

"There is none," replied Sarah Brown. "This is the House of Living Alone."

Miss Ford was pouring a grain or two of the magic into her palm. "How very credulous people are," she said with a self-conscious smile. "If Thelma Bennett Watkins were here she would credit this powder with--"

She stopped, for an astonishing sharp smell filled the Shop. Almost immediately a curious wheezy sound, punctuated by taps, proceeded from the corner. It was Mr. Bernard Tovey trying to sing, "Mon coeur s'ouvr' a ta voix," and beating time by swinging his heels against the counter on which he sat.

Sarah Brown felt suddenly well. She trembled but was well. She jumped off the counter. "I will run across, if you like," she said, "and ring up Richard from the ferryman's house. He may have left his True Love now. I am not deaf on the tele phone, and the ferryman won't admit strangers."

As she left, the smell of magic was getting stronger and stronger. Mr. Tovey, still impersonating Delilah in the corner, was approaching the more excitable passages of the song. Miss Ford was saying, "Really, Bernard...." Sarah Brown felt a slight misgiving.

A warm and rather dramatic-looking light was shining behind the red curtain of the ferryman's lattice window, as Sarah Brown crossed the moonlit road. She de-lighted, after her recent black hours, to think of all those people in the world who were sitting stuffily and pleasantly in little ugly rooms that they loved, doing quiet careful things that pleased them. And she told herself that the thought of Richard's little office, alone and alight in the deserted City every night, would comfort her often in the darkness.

The ferryman opened his door, and invited her genially to his telephone. He had been sitting at his table, surrounded by the snakes that for him took the place of a family. On the table was a bowl of milk from which a large bull-snake, in a gay Turkey-carpet design, was drinking. A yellow and black python lay coiled in sev-eral figures of eight in the armchair, and an intelligent-looking small dust-coloured snake with a broad nose and an active tongue leaned out of the ferryman's breast pocket.

"Aren't they beautiful?" he said, with shy and paternal pride, as Sarah Brown tried to find a place on which the python would like to be tickled or scratched. Somehow the python has a barren figure, from a caresser's point of view. The ferry-man went on: "There is something about the grip and spring in a snake's body that makes me feel giddy with pleasure. Snakes to me, you know, are just a drug, sold by the yard instead of in bottles. My brain is getting every day colder and quieter, and all through loving snakes so."

Sarah Brown rang up Richard's office, and the over-refined voice of a young gentleman clerk answered her.

Mr. Higgins was not in the office.

Mr. Higgins had left particular word that if any one wanted him they were to be told that he had--er--gone to his True Love.

But any minor business matter connected with magic could be attended to in his absence. Mr. Higgins spending so much of his time on the battlefield at pres-ent, a good deal of the routine work had to be done in any case by the speaker, his confidential clerk.

Passports to America? Perfectly simple. The office had simply to issue blank sheets treated in a certain way, and every official to whom the sheet should be presented would read upon it what he would want. But Mr. Higgins would have to affix his mark and seal. Mr. Higgins would be in the office sometime to-night, probably within the hour.

How many passports?

"Two," said Sarah Brown. "One for my friend and one for me. A dog doesn't need one, does he--a British dog? I will book the berths to-morrow. I can pawn my--or rather, I can sell my War Loan."

As she hung up the receiver, the ferryman asked: "Are you having a party up at the Shop, in the superintendent's absence?"

"Not intentionally," replied Sarah Brown. "Why?"

"Well, I just wondered. There's a noise like a thousand mad gramophones playing backwards, coming from there."

Sarah Brown's misgivings returned like a clap of thunder. She rushed back to the Shop.

The lantern was standing in the middle of the floor, its glass was shattered, and out of each of its eight panels streamed a great flame six or seven feet high, like the petal of an enormous flower. Facing these flames stood Miss Ford and Mr. Tovey, hand in hand, each singing a different song very earnestly. Lady Arabel had found somewhere a patent fire extinguisher, and was putting on her glasses in order to read the directions. Mr. Frere was hesitating in the background with a leaking biscuit tin full of water. The Mayor was gone.

"Great Scott!" said Sarah Brown. You'll burn the place down. Look at that row of petticoats up there, catching fire already. What have you done with the Mayor?"

"We made him invisible by mistake," whispered Mr. Tovey. "But sh--sh, he doesn't know it yet."

"Nothing matters," said Miss Ford. "We are all going to America." And she continued her song, which was an extempore one about the sea.

"But that's no reason why you should burn the house down," said Sarah Brown.

"That's what I thought," agreed Mr. Frere. "But water won't put out that flame."

The singers fell silent. Only the voice of the invisible Mayor could be heard, singing, "If those lips could only speak," in a loud tremulous voice, to the accompaniment of his own unseen stamping feet.

"You've been putting magic into that flame," said Sarah Brown distractedly. "I told you it was dangerous. Nothing will put magic out, except more magic. What will the witch say?"

"It doesn't matter what anybody says," said Miss Ford. "We are all going to America. No place and no person matters when I am not there. There are no places and no people existing where I am not. I have suspected it before, and now I am sure that everything is all a pretence, except me. Look how easy it was to dismiss that gross grocer from sight. He was just a bit of background. I have painted him out."

The drapery department on the ceiling was ablaze now, and flakes of ashy petticoat, and the metal frames of buttons, showered to the floor.

"I will go and get help," said Sarah Brown, and hurried out of doors, followed feverishly by David, who was not a very brave dog in moments of crisis, and yet liked to appear busy and helpful. It was to the ferryman's telephone that they returned. Sarah Brown knew that the fire was a magic fire, and that an appeal to the L.C.C. Fire Brigade would only bring defeat and unnecessary bewilderment upon a deserving organisation.

Sarah Brown rang up Richard's office, and Richard, who had a heroic and almost cinematic gift for being on hand at the right moments, answered her himself.

"Come at once," said Sarah Brown. "The House of Living Alone is on fire. Someone has been tampering with the magic drawer."

"Oh deah, deah," said Richard. "And this is such a busy night at the office too. Do you think it is really important? It is my house, you know."

"Well, I don't see what is to prevent Mitten Island from being burnt to the water's edge. In fact I don't see why, being a magic fire, it should stop at the water's edge. Not to mention that the Mayor----"

"Very well, I'll come," said Richard.

As she stepped out of the door he arrived.

"I came by flash of lightning," he explained, smoothing his hair and readjusting his Bill Sykes service cap, in the manner of one who has moved swiftly. "The lightning service is getting very bad. I was held up for quite three-quarters of a second over Whitehall. There was some wireless war-news coming in, and the lightning had to let it pass. Now, what's all this fuss about, Sarah Brown?"

There was a crowd of delirious Mitten Islanders round the House of Living Alone. While Sarah Brown and Richard were about fifty yards away, a many-forked and enormous white flame suddenly wrapped the house about, like a hand clutching and crushing it.

"The faggots round the stake are lighted," said Richard. "But the witch has fled."

It seemed that the stars were devoured by the flame, so far did it outshine them. The flame shrank in upon itself and collapsed. There was no more House of Living Alone.

"Oh, Richard," said Sarah Brown. "Your mother and Miss Ford and----"

"Was mother in there?" asked Richard placidly. "Wonders will never cease. Well, well, it is fortunate that no magic of any sort could ever touch mother."

And indeed, as they pushed through the crowd, they saw all the recent occupants of the Shop arguing at the front gate.

"I didn't blow it," Mr. Tovey was saying in an aggrieved voice. "I was singing, not blowing."

"Well, all I know is that while you were on that high note something seemed to scatter the flames, and the drawer full of explosives caught fire," said Mr. Darnby Frere aggressively, flourishing his empty biscuit tin.

"It doesn't matter," said Miss Ford calmly. "We are all going across the sea to-morrow." She roused herself a little, and said to Mr. Frere with a smile: "You know, I inherit the sea tradition. My father commanded H.M.S. *Indigestible* in '84."

"I wonder what put out the flame so suddenly?" asked Mr. Tovey, who was still dreamily beating time to imaginary music with one hand.

"I put it out," said Richard.

"I wonder whose house it is?" added Mr. Tovey, turning vaguely to face Richard.

"It is my house," said Richard.

They all discovered his presence.

"Your house, dear Rrchud?" exclaimed Lady Arabel. "Are you sure? I didn't know the Higginses had any house property on Mitten Island."

"They haven't now," replied Richard. "But never mind. It has always seemed to me that there were too many houses in the world. Most houses are traps into which everything enters, and out of which nothing comes. It always grieves me to see tradesmen pouring sustenance in at the back door, and no result or justification coming out of the front door. I often think that only the houses that men's bodies have deserted are really inhabited."

"It was I who burnt your house down, Richard," said Miss Ford. "But it doesn't matter. It wasn't a real house."

"You are right," said Richard. "To such as you, dear Meta, it was not a real house. It was the House of Living Alone, and only to people who live alone was it real. It is dark and deserted now, and levelled with the cold ground; it is as though it were a tent, being moved from its position to follow the fortunes of those dwellers alone who wander continually in silence up and down the world...."

He looked at Sarah Brown.

"Talking of wandering," said Miss Ford. "We are all going to America, Richard. Can you get us passports?"

"Certainly," agreed Richard. "To America, eh? A nice little trip for you all. America, you know, would be entirely magic, if it weren't for the Americans...."

"I have quite a circle of friends in New York," said Miss Ford, who seemed to be recovering from her nerve-storm.

"Beware," said Richard, "lest you all forget the magic of to-night, and change from adventurers to tourists."

"I am not going to America," said Lady Arabel. "I am going home. I never heard such dretful nonsense. I was only in fun when I agreed to the plan."

"I never agreed to the plan at all," said Mr. Frere. "I shall be truly thankful to get to bed, and wake up to-morrow sober. I will never go out to tea in Kensington again if this is the result."

"I am going to America," said Mr. Tovey, fixing his innocent eyes, obscured by hair, upon Miss Ford.

"I am going to America," echoed the unseen Mayor from an unexpected direction. Nobody had yet dared to tell him of the misfortune that had overtaken him. "I'll give up this Mayor job to-morrer. Catch me stayin' be'ind if--oh, by the way, that reminds me----"

"I didn't need reminding," interrupted Sarah Brown. "It seems to me that everybody has forgotten why they came here. Please, Richard, do you know of a spell to find a missing person?"

"Yes, several," answered Richard, who was always as eager as a travelling sales-man to recommend his wares. "There is an awfully ingenious little spell I can show you, if you happen to have a telephone book and a compass and a toad's heart and a hair from a black goat's beard about you. Or again, if you stand on a sea-beach at low tide on Christmas night with the moon at your back and a wax candle in your left hand, and write upon the sand the name--by the way, who is it you want to find?"

"The witch," answered Sarah Brown.

Richard's face fell. "Oh, only the witch?" he said. "I can tell you where she is without any spell at all. She's with my True Love at Higgins Farm, helping--oh, by the way, mother, I forgot to tell you. You are a grandmother."

"RRCHUD!" said Lady Arabel. She sat down suddenly on the smooth grass slope between the road and the garden hedge. "Ah, it is too cruel," she cried, bury-ing her face in her hands. "It is too cruel. Is this my son? I meant so well, and all my life I did the things that other people did, the natural things. Except just once. And for that once, I am so cruelly punished.... I am given a son who is no son to me, who says only things I mustn't understand ... who does only things I mustn't see...." She paused, and, taking her hands from her face, looked round aghast at Richard, who was sitting beside her on the bank, stroking her arm. "*A faery son* ..." she added in a terrified whisper, and then broke out again crying: "Ah, it is too cruel...."

Richard continued to stroke her arm without comprehension. "Yes, mother, and Peony, my True Love, insists on calling him Elbert," he said. "Mother, listen, Elbert your faery grandson...."

But Lady Arabel still sobbed.

CHAPTER X
THE DWELLER ALONE

Well, Sarah Brown, here we are," said the witch, her Byronic hair flying as she sat perilously on the rail of the deck. The distant flying buttresses of New York were supporting a shining sky, and north and east lay the harbour and sea, and many ships moving with the glad gait of home-comers after perilous voyaging.

Every minute upon the sea is a magic minute, but the voyage of the witch and Sarah Brown had been unmarked by any supernatural activities on the part of the witch. She had been more or less extinguished by the presence of five hundred Americans, not one of whom had ever heard the word "magic" used, except by advertisers in connection with their wares.

Miss Ford had been left behind, cured for ever of nerve-storms. She had become unexpectedly engaged to Mr. Bernard Tovey while looking for a porter on Lime Street Station, Liverpool, and had returned with him to London to celebrate the event by means of a Super-Wednesday. The Mayor also had failed to embark. Indeed the unfortunate man had not been heard of since his seizure on the night of the fire, and I believe that the London police are still trying to arrest him as a German spy.

"Here we are," said the witch to Sarah Brown. "At least, I suppose this City on its Tiptoes is New York. Do you think I ought to call the attention of the Captain to that largish lady on our left, who seems to be marooned upon a rock, and signalling to us for help?"

"That is the Statue of Liberty," said three neighbouring Americans in chorus.

"How d'you mean--Liberty?" asked the witch.

The three Americans froze her with three glances.

"America is the home of Liberty," they said all together.

"Oh yes, of course, how stupid of me," said the witch. "I ought to have remembered that every country is the Home of Liberty. Such a pity that Liberty never seems to begin at home. Every big shop in London, you know, is labelled Patronised by Royalty, yet I have bought haberdashery by the hour without running across a single queen. I suppose if you didn't have this big label sticking up in your harbour, you Americans might forget that America is the Home of Liberty. I know quite a lot about America from a grey squirrel who rents my may-tree on Mitten Island. It is a long time since he came over, but he still chitters with a strong New England accent. He came away because he was a socialist. I gather America is too full of Liberty to leave room for socialism, isn't that so? My squirrel says there are only two parties in America, Republicans and Sinners--at least I think that was what he said--and anybody who belongs to neither of these parties is given penal servitude for life. So I understood, but I may be wrong. I am not very good at politics. Anyway, my squirrel had to leave the Home of Liberty and come to England, so as to be able to say what he thought. I wish I were there too. Sarah Brown, I don't yet know why you brought me here."

"I brought you here to escape the Law," said Sarah Brown.

"How d'you mean--escape the Law? Didn't you know that all magic lives and thrives on the wrath of the Law? Have you forgotten our heroic tradition of martyrdom and the stake? Isn't the world tame enough already? What do you want Magic to become? A branch of the Civil Service?"

"I spent all I had in bringing you here," said Sarah Brown. "I left all I loved to bring you here. I am as if dead in England now. Nobody there will ever think of me again, except as a thing that has been heard the last of."

The witch looked kindly at her. "You know," she said, "when you first told me to go away, after Harold made that bad landing on a policeman, I thought perhaps you were a sort of cinema villainess, driving me away from my house and heritage. At first I thought of arguing the matter, but then I remembered that villains always have a rotten time, without being bullied and persecuted by the rest of us. Besides solid things are never worth fighting over. So I have been patient with you all this time, and have fallen in courteously with all your fiendish plans--as I thought--and now I am glad I was patient, for I see you meant well. Dear Sarah Brown, you did mean well. How sad it is that people who have once lived in the House of Living Alone can never make a success of friendship. You say you left all you loved--what business have you with love? Thank you, my dear, for meaning so well, and for these fair days at sea. But I mustn't stay with you. I mustn't set foot on this land--I can smell cleverness and un-magic even from here. I must go back to my little Spring island, and my parish of Faery...."

"Ah, witch, don't leave me, don't leave me like this, ill and bewildered and so far from home...."

"How can you ever be far from home, you, a dweller in the greatest home of all. Did you think you had destroyed the House of Living Alone? Did you think you could escape from it?"

Sarah Brown said nothing. She watched the witch call Harold her Broomstick to her, and adjust the saddle and tighten the strap round his middle. She watched her mount and embark upon the sunny air. The three Americans were talking politics, and did not notice anything but each other. The witch alighted for a moment on one spike of the crown of Liberty, and climbing carefully down on to the lady's parting, was seen by Sarah Brown to bend down till her head hung apoplectically upside down, and gaze long and curiously into that impassive bronze eye. Presently she remounted Harold, and, with a flippant and ambiguous gesture of her foot, launched herself eastward. She disappeared without looking back.

The dock was reached. Sarah Brown collected David her Dog, and Humphrey her Suit-case. Hers was a very wieldy family. An official asked her something, using one side of his mouth only to do so, in the alarming manner of American officials.

"I cannot hear you," said Sarah Brown. "I am stone deaf."

And she stepped over the threshold of the greater House of Living Alone.

The Codes Of Hammurabi And Moses
W. W. Davies

QTY

The discovery of the Hammurabi Code is one of the greatest achievements of archaeology, and is of paramount interest, not only to the student of the Bible, but also to all those interested in ancient history...

Religion   **ISBN:** *1-59462-338-4*   **Pages:132**
MSRP $12.95

The Theory of Moral Sentiments
Adam Smith

QTY

This work from 1749. contains original theories of conscience amd moral judgment and it is the foundation for systemof morals.

Philosophy   **ISBN:** *1-59462-777-0*   **Pages:536**
MSRP $19.95

Jessica's First Prayer
Hesba Stretton

QTY

In a screened and secluded corner of one of the many railway-bridges which span the streets of London there could be seen a few years ago, from five o'clock every morning until half past eight, a tidily set-out coffee-stall, consisting of a trestle and board, upon which stood two large tin cans, with a small fire of charcoal burning under each so as to keep the coffee boiling during the early hours of the morning when the work-people were thronging into the city on their way to their daily toil...

Pages:84

Childrens   **ISBN:** *1-59462-373-2*   *MSRP $9.95*

My Life and Work
Henry Ford

QTY

Henry Ford revolutionized the world with his implementation of mass production for the Model T automobile. Gain valuable business insight into his life and work with his own auto-biography... "We have only started on our development of our country we have not as yet, with all our talk of wonderful progress, done more than scratch the surface. The progress has been wonderful enough but..."

Pages:300

Biographies/   **ISBN:** *1-59462-198-5*   *MSRP $21.95*

The Art of Cross-Examination
Francis Wellman

QTY

I presume it is the experience of every author, after his first book is published upon an important subject, to be almost overwhelmed with a wealth of ideas and illustrations which could readily have been included in his book, and which to his own mind, at least, seem to make a second edition inevitable. Such certainly was the case with me; and when the first edition had reached its sixth impression in five months, I rejoiced to learn that it seemed to my publishers that the book had met with a sufficiently favorable reception to justify a second and considerably enlarged edition. ...

Pages:412

Reference   ISBN: *1-59462-647-2*   *MSRP $19.95*

On the Duty of Civil Disobedience
Henry David Thoreau

QTY

Thoreau wrote his famous essay, On the Duty of Civil Disobedience, as a protest against an unjust but popular war and the immoral but popular institution of slave-owning. He did more than write—he declined to pay his taxes, and was hauled off to gaol in consequence. Who can say how much this refusal of his hastened the end of the war and of slavery ?

Law   ISBN: *1-59462-747-9*   **Pages:48**

MSRP $7.45

Dream Psychology Psychoanalysis for Beginners
Sigmund Freud

QTY

Sigmund Freud, born Sigismund Schlomo Freud (May 6, 1856 - September 23, 1939), was a Jewish-Austrian neurologist and psychiatrist who co-founded the psychoanalytic school of psychology. Freud is best known for his theories of the unconscious mind, especially involving the mechanism of repression; his redefinition of sexual desire as mobile and directed towards a wide variety of objects; and his therapeutic techniques, especially his understanding of transference in the therapeutic relationship and the presumed value of dreams as sources of insight into unconscious desires.

Dream Psychology
Psychoanalysis for Beginners

Sigmund Freud

Pages:196

Psychology   ISBN: *1-59462-905-6*   *MSRP $15.45*

The Miracle of Right Thought
Orison Swett Marden

QTY

Believe with all of your heart that you will do what you were made to do. When the mind has once formed the habit of holding cheerful, happy, prosperous pictures, it will not be easy to form the opposite habit. It does not matter how improbable or how far away this realization may see, or how dark the prospects may be, if we visualize them as best we can, as vividly as possible, hold tenaciously to them and vigorously struggle to attain them, they will gradually become actualized, realized in the life. But a desire, a longing without endeavor, a yearning abandoned or held indifferently will vanish without realization.

Pages:360

Self Help   ISBN: *1-59462-644-8*   *MSRP $25.45*

www.**bookjungle**.com *email: sales@bookjungle.com fax: 630-214-0564 mail: Book Jungle PO Box 2226 Champaign, IL 61825*

QTY

The Rosicrucian Cosmo-Conception Mystic Christianity by *Max Heindel*   ISBN: *1-59462-188-8* **$38.95**
The Rosicrucian Cosmo-conception is not dogmatic, neither does it appeal to any other authority than the reason of the student. It is: not controversial, but is: sent forth in the, hope that it may help to clear...   New Age/Religion Pages 646

Abandonment To Divine Providence by *Jean-Pierre de Caussade*   ISBN: *1-59462-228-0* **$25.95**
"The Rev. Jean Pierre de Caussade was one of the most remarkable spiritual writers of the Society of Jesus in France in the 18th Century. His death took place at Toulouse in 1751. His works have gone through many editions and have been republished...   Inspirational/Religion Pages 400

Mental Chemistry by *Charles Haanel*   ISBN: *1-59462-192-6* **$23.95**
Mental Chemistry allows the change of material conditions by combining and appropriately utilizing the power of the mind. Much like applied chemistry creates something new and unique out of careful combinations of chemicals the mastery of mental chemistry...   New Age Pages 354

The Letters of Robert Browning and Elizabeth Barret Barrett 1845-1846 vol II   ISBN: *1-59462-193-4* **$35.95**
by *Robert Browning* and *Elizabeth Barrett*   Biographies Pages 596

Gleanings In Genesis (volume I) by *Arthur W. Pink*   ISBN: *1-59462-130-6* **$27.45**
Appropriately has Genesis been termed "the seed plot of the Bible" for in it we have, in germ form, almost all of the great doctrines which are afterwards fully developed in the books of Scripture which follow...   Religion/Inspirational Pages 420

The Master Key by *L. W. de Laurence*   ISBN: *1-59462-001-6* **$30.95**
In no branch of human knowledge has there been a more lively increase of the spirit of research during the past few years than in the study of Psychology, Concentration and Mental Discipline. The requests for authentic lessons in Thought Control, Mental Discipline and...   New Age/Business Pages 422

The Lesser Key Of Solomon Goetia by *L. W. de Laurence*   ISBN: *1-59462-092-X* **$9.95**
This translation of the first book of the "Lernegton" which is now for the first time made accessible to students of Talismanic Magic was done, after careful collation and edition, from numerous Ancient Manuscripts in Hebrew, Latin, and French...   New Age/Occult Pages 92

Rubaiyat Of Omar Khayyam by *Edward Fitzgerald*   ISBN:*1-59462-332-5* **$13.95**
Edward Fitzgerald, whom the world has already learned, in spite of his own efforts to remain within the shadow of anonymity, to look upon as one of the rarest poets of the century, was born at Bredfield, in Suffolk, on the 31st of March, 1809. He was the third son of John Purcell...   Music Pages 172

Ancient Law by *Henry Maine*   ISBN: *1-59462-128-4* **$29.95**
The chief object of the following pages is to indicate some of the earliest ideas of mankind, as they are reflected in Ancient Law, and to point out the relation of those ideas to modern thought.   Religion/History Pages 452

Far-Away Stories by *William J. Locke*   ISBN: *1-59462-129-2* **$19.45**
"Good wine needs no bush, but a collection of mixed vintages does. And this book is just such a collection. Some of the stories I do not want to remain buried for ever in the museum files of dead magazine-numbers an author's not unpardonable vanity..."   Fiction Pages 272

Life of David Crockett by *David Crockett*   ISBN: *1-59462-250-7* **$27.45**
"Colonel David Crockett was one of the most remarkable men of the times in which he lived. Born in humble life, but gifted with a strong will, an indomitable courage, and unremitting perseverance...   Biographies/New Age Pages 424

Lip-Reading by *Edward Nitchie*   ISBN: *1-59462-206-X* **$25.95**
Edward B. Nitchie, founder of the New York School for the Hard of Hearing, now the Nitchie School of Lip-Reading, Inc, wrote "LIP-READING Principles and Practice". The development and perfecting of this meritorious work on lip-reading was an undertaking...   How-to Pages 400

A Handbook of Suggestive Therapeutics, Applied Hypnotism, Psychic Science   ISBN: *1-59462-214-0* **$24.95**
by *Henry Munro*   Health/New Age/Health/Self-help Pages 376

A Doll's House: and Two Other Plays by *Henrik Ibsen*   ISBN: *1-59462-112-8* **$19.95**
Henrik Ibsen created this classic when in revolutionary 1848 Rome. Introducing some striking concepts in playwriting for the realist genre, this play has been studied the world over.   Fiction/Classics/Plays 308

The Light of Asia by *sir Edwin Arnold*   ISBN: *1-59462-204-3* **$13.95**
In this poetic masterpiece, Edwin Arnold describes the life and teachings of Buddha. The man who was to become known as Buddha to the world was born as Prince Gautama of India but he rejected the worldly riches and abandoned the reigns of power when...   Religion/History/Biographies Pages 170

The Complete Works of Guy de Maupassant by *Guy de Maupassant*   ISBN: *1-59462-157-8* **$16.95**
"For days and days, nights and nights, I had dreamed of that first kiss which was to consecrate our engagement, and I knew not on what spot I should put my lips..."   Fiction/Classics Pages 240

The Art of Cross-Examination by *Francis L. Wellman*   ISBN: *1-59462-309-0* **$26.95**
Written by a renowned trial lawyer, Wellman imparts his experience and uses case studies to explain how to use psychology to extract desired information through questioning.   How-to/Science/Reference Pages 408

Answered or Unanswered? by *Louisa Vaughan*   ISBN: *1-59462-248-5* **$10.95**
Miracles of Faith in China   Religion Pages 112

The Edinburgh Lectures on Mental Science (1909) by *Thomas*   ISBN: *1-59462-008-3* **$11.95**
This book contains the substance of a course of lectures recently given by the writer in the Queen Street Hall, Edinburgh. Its purpose is to indicate the Natural Principles governing the relation between Mental Action and Material Conditions...   New Age/Psychology Pages 148

Ayesha by *H. Rider Haggard*   ISBN: *1-59462-301-5* **$24.95**
Verily and indeed it is the unexpected that happens! Probably if there was one person upon the earth from whom the Editor of this, and of a certain previous history, did not expect to hear again...   Classics Pages 380

Ayala's Angel by *Anthony Trollope*   ISBN: *1-59462-352-X* **$29.95**
The two girls were both pretty, but Lucy who was twenty-one who supposed to be simple and comparatively unattractive, whereas Ayala was credited, as her Bombwhat romantic name might show, with poetic charm and a taste for romance. Ayala when her father died was nineteen...   Fiction Pages 484

The American Commonwealth by *James Bryce*   ISBN: *1-59462-286-8* **$34.45**
An interpretation of American democratic political theory. It examines political mechanics and society from the perspective of Scotsman James Bryce   Politics Pages 572

Stories of the Pilgrims by *Margaret P. Pumphrey*   ISBN: *1-59462-116-0* **$17.95**
This book explores pilgrims religious oppression in England as well as their escape to Holland and eventual crossing to America on the Mayflower, and their early days in New England...   History Pages 268

www.bookjungle.com *email: sales@bookjungle.com fax: 630-214-0564 mail: Book Jungle PO Box 2226 Champaign, IL 61825*

QTY

The Fasting Cure *by Sinclair Upton*   ISBN: *1-59462-222-1* **$13.95**
In the Cosmopolitan Magazine for May, 1910, and in the Contemporary Review (London) for April, 1910, I published an article dealing with my experiences in fasting. I have written a great many magazine articles, but never one which attracted so much attention... New Age/Self Help/Health Pages 164

Hebrew Astrology *by Sepharial*   ISBN: *1-59462-308-2* **$13.45**
In these days of advanced thinking it is a matter of common observation that we have left many of the old landmarks behind and that we are now pressing forward to greater heights and to a wider horizon than that which represented the mind-content of our progenitors...   Astrology Pages 144

Thought Vibration or The Law of Attraction in the Thought World   ISBN: *1-59462-127-6* **$12.95**
by William Walker Atkinson   *Psychology/Religion Pages 144*

Optimism *by Helen Keller*   ISBN: *1-59462-108-X* **$15.95**
Helen Keller was blind, deaf, and mute since 19 months old, yet famously learned how to overcome these handicaps, communicate with the world, and spread her lectures promoting optimism. An inspiring read for everyone...   Biographies/Inspirational Pages 84

Sara Crewe *by Frances Burnett*   ISBN: *1-59462-360-0* **$9.45**
In the first place, Miss Minchin lived in London. Her home was a large, dull, tall one, in a large, dull square, where all the houses were alike, and all the sparrows were alike, and where all the door-knockers made the same heavy sound...   Childrens/Classic Pages 88

The Autobiography of Benjamin Franklin *by Benjamin Franklin*   ISBN: *1-59462-135-7* **$24.95**
The Autobiography of Benjamin Franklin has probably been more extensively read than any other American historical work, and no other book of its kind has had such ups and downs of fortune. Franklin lived for many years in England, where he was agent...   Biographies/History Pages 332

Name	
Email	
Telephone	
Address	
City, State ZIP	

☐ **Credit Card**   ☐ **Check / Money Order**

Credit Card Number	
Expiration Date	
Signature	

Please Mail to: Book Jungle
PO Box 2226
Champaign, IL 61825
or Fax to: 630-214-0564

ORDERING INFORMATION

web: *www.bookjungle.com*
email: *sales@bookjungle.com*
fax: *630-214-0564*
mail: *Book Jungle PO Box 2226 Champaign, IL 61825*
or PayPal *to sales@bookjungle.com*

Please contact us for bulk discounts

DIRECT-ORDER TERMS

20% Discount if You Order Two or More Books
Free Domestic Shipping!
Accepted: Master Card, Visa, Discover, American Express

www.ingramcontent.com/pod-product-compliance
Lightning Source LLC
Chambersburg PA
CBHW080748250626
47162CB00010B/3058